Absolution

Stories

Timothy Jacques Maynard

First Edition

PAGE PUBLISHING
Conneaut Lake, PA

First originally published by Page Publishing 2024

ISBN 979-8-89315-106-0 (pbk)
ISBN 979-8-89315-124-4 (digital)

Printed in the United States of America

These stories are dedicated to my
parents, Jacques and Velma Maynard,
who helped form them.

Contents

The Vast Silent Sea

The brothers met at the marina in the Great Salt Pond of Block Island, Rhode Island, at sunrise. Ned's boat, Marigold, was berthed at Payne's Dock in a slip that had been occupied by a James family member since their grandfather first discovered the location when he returned, spent and sad, from the Korean War. Marigold was a twin-engine Back Cove 29, a fine new boat that looked like a sleek down-easter. A lobsterman wouldn't be caught dead in her. It was a fiberglass pleasure craft built for fishing, swimming, and comfort. Like most private boats, she spent her time waiting for the master to show up while spending her owner's money on dock fees, maintenance, and mortgage. Now in late July, Marigold was going to sea for only the third trip of the season.

"I wasn't sure you were going to make it this morning, Ned."

Slamming the door of his pickup, Ned took a last, long draw on his Marlboro and threw it into a pile of drying quahog shells. “When have I ever missed an opportunity to fish with my big brother?”

Jack said, “2018, 2017, 2016. I could keep going, all the way back to 1985.”

“Aw, come on now. I’ve been busy. It takes a lot of cash to keep Grampa’s legacy intact.”

“No, it just takes a boatload of Seagram’s Seven. You’ve done a fine job.”

“Psha.” Ned changed the subject. “It looks like a great day to catch a tuna. Beautiful sky. Look at that crimson sunrise. It’s like blood. Bloody beautiful.”

Jack sighed, “So you own a fishing boat, and you want to keep Grampa’s legacy alive, but you don’t know he always said, ‘Red sky at night, sailors’ delight. Red sky in the morning, sailors take warning’?”

“Sure. Gramps and Dad taught me those old fisherman yarns. But Mom taught me to read. Marine weather says there will be a few minor squalls off Newport, nothing to worry about. We will be heading south. Flat seas.”

Jack saluted. “Okay, Captain. So what we waiting for? I’m ready.”

“Yeah, so ready, you already have sunscreen on before sunup.”

“Scout. Remember ‘Be prepared’?”

The dark sky began to shift from deep red to flamingo pink. The flashing harbor navigation buoys lost their intensity.

Ned said, "Boy Scouts, so last century. Anyway, I'm waiting for Payne's to open. Best coffee on the Block at zero five thirty in the a.m. The only coffee at zero five thirty. In two minutes, Candace should be unlocking her doors."

"You've been waiting for her to do that since 2000, bro."

Ned winked and said, "2015, bro."

"No…"

"Yes, so shut up."

Just then, the creaky dockside marina door opened, and the sign flipped from Closed to Welcome to the Block. Ned offered, "What took so long, Candace?"

"I should ask you the same thing."

As they exchanged mocking glances, Jack took over. "Hi, Candace. Two large coffees, black. How's the family?"

"Good. Everything good. How is Dani?" replied Candace.

"Fine," said Jack. "She and the kids are at the Spring House for a few days. I'm sure they are happy to have a day to explore the Block without us. Tell your ma we said hello."

"I will. You do the same. Where you headed today?"

"Ned has the crazy idea bluefin tuna still exist. We are going to the Southwest Ledge toward the Gulfstream for the hunt."

"Ted Williams caught a three hundred pounder there in 1961," Ned said. "Why can't we?"

"Because that was so last century," Jack said. "And it was 557 pounds. Thanks for the coffee, Candace. If we aren't back by midnight, it's Ned's fault."

"We can't be sure of that, but what are the odds?" said Candace. "Take care of each other. Have fun, boys."

Marigold and crew slipped away from the dock and idled out of the Great Salt Pond with remnants of the pink and blue sunrise reflecting off the tidal shoals. The brothers passed the number two red harbor buoy in silence and pointed Marigold southwest toward the wide Atlantic Ocean, bringing her up to a smooth twelve knots with a light ocean swell and soft westerly breezes. When they arrived near the Southwest Ledge, a commercial trawler slowly mined the sea for treasure. Seagulls swarmed around the stern. The stench from the boat drove Ned to point his boat due south. They were looking for quiet, peaceful hunting.

By 9:00 a.m., Jack and Ned were far off the coast, far from Rhode Island, far from civilization. When Ned cut the engine, the silence disrupted their normal sense of living, with no city hums and no highway traffic. The only noise was the occasional lap of waves against the boat and the occasional churn of the automatic bilge pump. As the boat rose with the ocean swells, they could sometimes see the tops of blades from the offshore wind farm southeast of Block Island.

Together they prepared their fishing lures, dropped two lines into the deep. Ned popped open two Narragansett Beers.

"Hey, thanks, Ned."

"What do you mean? These are both for me. Get your own." Waiting for a reaction and receiving none, he handed a beer to his big brother. "Just kidding. Bro. Like old times."

"Thanks again. Here's to old times."

"Last century. Cheers."

As the breeze and swell pushed them southward and eastward, they sat on the flying bridge enjoying the solitude, the vast expanse of blue green sea and bright sky in all directions interrupted only by the yellow midmorning sun in the east and a line of building thunderclouds far to the west. In this peace, they had a respite from their brotherly bickering. The vast sea was silent.

Great tuna tournaments were held out of Rhode Island before commercial overfishing depleted the stock. The last ten years of the event yielded no giant bluefins, so the tournament folded when Jack and Ned were still teens. To catch a fish larger than a hundred pounds today required a combination of location, luck, bait, and a modest amount of skill. Mostly luck. Remnants of the Gulf Stream came close to New England's southern coast. The fishermen could lie dead in the water and let the deep-water flow push their bait. They could sit and wait for something to happen. That was fishing. Sit and wait for the tug on the line.

The sea was peaceful. Immaculately silent. Vast. But Ned needed to break the spell. "So this is where we are at. Nothing to say to each other."

Jack replied, "What do you mean? I'm enjoying the peace and quiet. I don't need to say anything."

"Okay. I follow that. You do have something to say. You started at the docks. Didn't think I'd show. 2018, 2017, 2016. You have a problem with me?"

"No," said Jack.

"Bringing up Candace. Why you have to do that?"

"Huh? What's bugging you?" Jack said. "I didn't mean anything by it. I'm not judging. We live two separate lives. Yes, we are brothers. But that doesn't mean we need to hang out. Our life choices, our philosophies are different. It's not a problem. I get it."

"I've got nothing to apologize for," Ned said.

"I'm not asking for an apology. What is eating you?"

"What good is a boat that never sails? What good is a family that never eats together?"

"Whoa. Ned. I'm not a marriage counselor. You gotta take care of that yourself. With Catherine. I'm too far removed, and too close to your side as a brother, to be helpful."

Ned crushed his beer can between his hands and tossed it overboard. He lit a cigarette and blew the Marlboro smoke into the fresh sea air. "I'm sorry."

Jack watched the aluminum sink into the deep. He said, "I'm not the one who needs to forgive you, man. All I can say is look in the mirror."

"Shit. We are so different. Grampa always said so. You still believe in God, for Christ's sake."

"Hey. Yes, for Christ's sake. But not in a blasphemous way. At least I have a moral compass."

"Sorry."

"How did you get so far off course? Didn't you even buy into the Boy Scout stuff?"

"Damn. What has God, or the Boy Scouts, ever done for me?

"Seriously? Who do you think created the tuna we are hunting?"

"Ever hear of evolution? It's called science, Jack."

"Ugh. Evolution is called a theory for a reason. I wouldn't put all my faith in science. Where has that gotten you? There are things science will never figure out, things that just can't be proven."

"Whatever."

"There you go. You bring something up, then never finish once you actually have to think about it." They stopped talking. The gentle rocking of the boat moved the shadow from the Bimini Top back and forth across Ned's face.

"It's too quiet," said Ned. "Driving me crazy."

"This is your boat. Don't you have music?"

"Oh, yeah. We got something. Here we go. Jimmy Buffet. *Songs You Know by Heart*. We could also fire up the engines. Troll these fishing lines out."

"Roger that, Captain. I'll take care of that."

Jack started the engines, engaged idle speed, and set the autopilot to a northwest course, heading slowly back toward port. The noises reset the brothers' attitudes and halted their unfinished conversation.

As the brothers belted out "Son of a Son of a Sailor" along with Jimmy Buffet, they did not hear the pop of a catastrophic failure in the engine water cooling system or the auto-bilge pump engage.

When Jack headed down from the bridge to replenish the beers, he saw two feet of water covering the galley deck. He screamed, "Whoa, brother we got a big problem! We're sinking!" He ran immediately up to the deck and pulled open the engine compartment hatch. Seawater flushed into the engine room.

"What the? Oh my god, what's going on?" Ned thrust his head into the engine compartment and saw water pouring in. The stern was already noticeably low. "Jack! We are going down. Oh my god, shit!"

Jack seized the radio. "Mayday! Mayday! This is fishing vessel Marigold out of Block Island. We are sinking. Two souls on board. James brothers. We are thirty miles southwest. Correction. Thirty miles southeast of Block Island southeast light. Mayday. Mayday." His call was accompanied by Jimmy Buffet singing "Cheeseburger in Paradise." There was no response.

Jack began throwing anything that would float off the side of the boat. The seat cushions, the beer cooler, the life ring. He found four life jackets, put one on. He grabbed windbreaker jackets, long pants. Sunscreen. Hats. In a panic, Ned tried to climb into the engine compartment to find and stop the leak, but Jack pulled him back up.

"It's too late, Ned. This boat is going down. We need to get what we can. Take care of ourselves. Here. Put this on. Do you have any other fresh water? We have to get off real soon before she drags us under with her."

Ned scrambled into the bow compartment. He tightened the bow hatch as tight as possible. He grabbed loose items that might float. Two boat fenders, a piece of rope, a first aid kit, a waterproof bag. The boat hook.

As water continued to pour into the boat with the sea splashing at their knees, the two brothers met each other face to face.

"Anything else? Do you have a flare? Any more fresh water?"

"No flare. Just the water in the cooler. Make one more mayday!"

"Put that life vest on proper right now. We are going into the water. One more *mayday*, then we swim."

They made the call then they made the leap. Jack blessed himself before entering the Atlantic Ocean with his brother. It took only twelve minutes for Marigold to sink. As she went down stern first, an air pocket in the bow briefly held the boat in a vertical position just below the surface. The bow pennant, a Boston Red Sox flag, waved goodbye to the men as it sank slowly to the deep. Ned, crying, panicking, flailing in the sea, reached down to try to grab the flag. Then he turned his jumbled attention to swim toward the direction he thought the boat had been headed.

"Ned! Ned! Stop! Save your energy. Come here! Let's gather what floats." Jack held the life ring, an extra lifejacket, and the beer cooler.

"Oh god, oh god, oh god. What do we do? What do we do, Jack!" As the ocean swells rose around them, they swam to each other.

"Come here. Calm down. We stay together."

"We going to die. Oh god."

"Come on. We stay together. Someone heard our mayday. They will come looking. It's July. Water pretty warm, pretty calm."

Once they had gathered nearby floating pieces of the boat, the seat cushions, the fenders, the extra life jackets, they paused, caught their breath, rested.

The vast silence of the sea returned. They waited. Their field of view was much more restricted than being on the bridge of the Marigold. Now the hazy blue sky dominated, and the dark sea took on a greenish, pickled look below. They could only see into the distance when a swell raised them up. Neither could think what to say to the other until Ned said, "I thirst."

"Me too, brother. We have water and beer. I think we should stick with water. Maybe beer for when we get rescued. Here you go. We have four bottles. Take one."

"Thanks. Jack, you think we will make it?"

"Yes. We will make it."

"We're going to die, aren't we?"

"Yes."

"Shit."

"You asked, bro. Maybe this isn't the time to bring it up, but we are going to die. Maybe not today, but we all are going to die. That is why the scouts said be prepared."

"Okay, well, I want to confess to you. I did cheat on Catherine. Not just with Candace. A few more. I'm in debt over my head. And I…"

"Ned. Stop. You don't need to confess. Certainly not to me. Come on. Have hope. We are going to make it out of this."

"Yeah, but I wanna tell you. It's eating me alive. I'm a crappy husband. Catherine must know. Oh god. What do I do?"

"Relax and wait to be rescued," Jack said.

"How can we relax? My boat just sank. We're lost at sea. How can you be so calm? Damn it."

"I'll tell you my secret, brother. I'm prepared to die. You never know when a car accident might happen. Or you get mugged in the city. Heart attack. Or whatever. You gotta be prepared. No matter what happens, I have my family set. Insurance. Letters to the kids. And Dani. I always say goodbye to Mom like I will never see her again. I try to be ready to meet my maker. Every day. I'll tell you what, it keeps me out of trouble."

"Like the trouble we're in now?"

"Well. Yeah. I'm not really in trouble. I'm ready for this."

"Unbelievable. I'm not ready."

"If we make it out of this, you renew your life. Set your priorities. Get yourself prepared. To die. To live."

"Okay, okay. Got it. God. I love you, Jack."

"Love you too, Ned. You'll always be my brother."

In the vastness of Block Island Sound, only thirty miles from land, the brothers bobbed together, holding each other. The sun began to set, a jolly rouge.

"Red sky at night, sailors' delight."

In the darkness of the sea, the glow of city lights from New York and Providence lit the horizon with a pulsing orange glow, like there were blazing campfires far away. Directly above, a multitude of stars radiated upon the brothers. A rescue helicopter scanned the waters, hunting like fishermen. Jack and Ned spent the night huddled together, waiting to die or live, deep in the vast silent sea.

Notes from Elizabeth

It began on an icy day in November on the Upper West Side of Manhattan. Father Damian Antonio had a dutiful habit of strolling along Central Park West after daily Mass, but on that morning, the weather was too much for him. After only two blocks of slushy, unplowed snow, he abandoned his walk and slipped into Café Chien for coffee. The French bistro was quiet. The six tables, strategically spread out where there used to be twelve, were occupied by two businessmen, a couple using their cell phones, a young mother with a quiet baby, and a single, mid-twenty-year-old woman with auburn hair to her shoulders, dark eyes, and a fine mohair overcoat. She gracefully sipped her coffee from a black mug and her dark red lipstick pressed a half kiss onto the rim.

Damian, dressed in all black from head to shoes, except for the white Roman collar at his throat, stumbled past the businessmen and baby stroller to sit near the back, observing all but avoiding eye contact. He ordered a café au lait and *The Wall Street Journal.* His interest in the paper was the quick summary of headlines but, more importantly, as a sly way to divert attention away from an unwanted conversation should one of his overtalkative parishioners attempt to infiltrate his domain. He still wanted the benefit gained from his walk: thinking to himself, praying by himself, solitude. Perhaps the waitress did not understand and did not care much about social distance. All it seemed to do was cut into her tips. She delivered his coffee and newspaper. Through her mask she blurted, "Here you go, Father. Is there anything else? Some weather, huh? What a surprise this morning, am I right? Can I ask? What are you, like thirty-five? Who becomes a priest anymore? Just sayin'. It's awful quiet in the churches. Just sayin'."

Damian directed his blue eyes directly into her brown eyes, smiled wryly, and said nothing. For a moment, the server did not know what to say or do. She slinked away, finally quiet.

Elizabeth Norland, the woman in the elegant overcoat, scribbled on her paper napkin and stood to leave. She paused briefly at Damian's table without looking at him and gracefully left a note:

Powerful

\- - -

When morning Mass concluded at Saint Brigid's, as the congregation of fifteen departed, Damian noticed the same elegant lady with the burnt brown overcoat lingering in the last pew. By the time he extinguished the candles and removed his vestments in the sacristy, she was gone. Left at her seat was a note in soft, flowing script:

Strong

\- - -

Damian felt an unusually compelling urge to walk straight to Café Chien to see if she was there. He thought, *Why? What would I do? Powerfully stare? Would it be sinful?* No, he decided to take his morning walk as usual then get to work on parish business. He walked along the western edge of Central Park, trying to enjoy his solitude, trying to return his mind to his own thoughts and prayers. Instead, his mind kept wandering to her. His feet were drawn to the bistro as he convinced himself she may not necessarily be there, and he was only stopping for coffee.

Father Damian sat at a table across the café from her, heart thumping. He observed her graceful countenance, stylish clothes, her significant diamond on her ring finger. She, however, was preparing to leave. She reapplied her dark lipstick then dropped a note on his table as she departed:

Elizabeth

- - -

It only took two days for Damian, a complete novice at the game, to become obsessed. Her messages were brief, always enticing, his messages were sent by silently showing up. By the next week, Damian no longer walked along Central Park West. He sat, drank coffee, read the paper, said nothing, sometimes dared to look directly at Elizabeth, but the two did not converse. He just waited for his note. She sometimes had a book to read, sometimes answered her smartphone. This odd relationship only increased. Damian skipped going to see his mother in New Rochelle on his day off. He sat in the bistro, content, silent. Elizabeth seemed perfectly happy to have this same relationship. He sometimes spoke briefly to parishioners or others who initiated conversation but soon picked up his Wall Street prop and ended the talk. He saw other couples enter and sit together, order pastries and coffee, and not talk to each other. He thought about sitting with Elizabeth, like other couples, then realized this could jeopardize everything.

In the season of Advent, Damian preached about preparing for Christmas and the new year by receiving God's grace through confession. He reminded the parishioners that modern confessional rooms provided two methods of confession. The priest sat next to a traditional screen and the penitent could kneel or sit on the other side, obscuring identities. Alternatively, a person could sit face to face with the priest and confess. On Saturday afternoon, after the widows dutifully reported their sinful gossiping or semi-silent cursing, near the end of the designated time for confessions, Elizabeth entered the private side of the confessional. Damian perceived her fine perfume and the shimmering of her fashionable skirt. She knelt. She did not speak. The priest also remained silent, heart thumping. They remained this way, in the presence of God, for more than ten minutes until she finally, silently, departed.

On the evening of December 18, Saint Brigid parish held a Christmas reception in the parish hall. Children sang carols, parishioners carefully greeted each other. Father Damian dutifully greeted the families and thanked them for participating in parish activities. Cookies and punch were served, and Damian personally walked among the crowd to be kind to all. He tried to look at Elizabeth when he could but also endeavored to avoid her. Elizabeth walked close to Damian a few times but passed by him, just out of reach.

At one point, with Elizabeth safely at a distance, a man approached Damian. "Father, I am Raymond Norland, Elizabeth's husband. It is a pleasure to meet you. I hear you are sort of a playmate for my wife at the coffee shop. I'm sorry, I don't mean playmate. I mean friend. Playmate, that's rich."

Damian was flummoxed. First, he did not expect to speak to either Mrs. or Mr. Norland. Second, Raymond Norland was beautiful. If anyone could be more elegant than Elizabeth, he was the male version of style. His short-cropped, manicured haircut perfectly framed his sculpted jawline. His dark gray suit perfectly framed his muscular, long body. Damian fumbled to provide a pleasant response, and Elizabeth watched the exchange from across the hall.

Damian was determined to resume his morning hikes and the routine he had before she had entered his life. Of course, he could not. He knew she was married. He had seen her fine diamond and wedding band. He had just spoken to her husband. He thought, *What was her marriage? Why did she spend time with him? Was it a game? Was he a playmate on a series of playdates?* When he arrived at Café Chien,

Elizabeth was not there. His list of questions grew longer and wider. He sat in his usual seat and ordered his usual fare. In silent contemplation, he waited. The waitress delivered his coffee and his paper and "Oh, this came for you," handing him an envelope. He lowered his medical mask and held the envelope to his nose, breathing in the lavender scent, wondering how softly and kindly Elizabeth would be in ending the relationship. He did not want to read her explanation. He wondered if a simple disappearance would be less cruel than an explanation. He finished his coffee, generously tipped the waitress, and stepped to the cold sidewalk with his newspaper and unopened letter.

Damian returned to the church and sat in the pew that Elizabeth most often occupied. He closed his eyes, slipped his finger under the flap of the envelope, and opened it:

Because I am lonely
Noon, Natural History Museum

\---

Damian remained lost. Did it make sense that she was lonely? Perhaps he misinterpreted her beauty, and her husband's beauty, for happiness. He always saw she was alone, but it seemed she was happy in that state, as he was. Although her beauty and grace attracted many would-be friends, she always kindly rebuffed the advances. He remembered one occasion, as she sat in the café, when she tried to use his silent stare to repel an intruder. She was not as successful as he. She had to get up and leave, rolling her eyes at Damian.

He could not meet Elizabeth at the museum. It was not because he did not try to manically rearrange his schedule. A parishioner had been hit by a bus, and Damian was needed to administer last rites. He felt bad that he had to minister and bad that he missed his Elizabeth. The next day, without any hint of disappointment or need of explanation, they resumed their morning routine in Café Chien, separately, together.

On Christmas morning, Damian served Mass, preaching about love. As parishioners paraded out, passing greetings to each other, Elizabeth sweetly and quietly spoke to him, "Merry Christmas, Father Damian. I enjoyed your sermon. I understand."

It was like a kiss on the lips for Damian. Their protocol had been broken, as a Christmas present from Elizabeth. It was the grandest Christmas gift he could ever hope for. He responded in kind, saying her name out loud for the first time. He floated on his train ride to New Rochelle for Christmas dinner with his mother. He floated back to Manhattan. It was his favorite Christmas.

They were at Café Chien the next day, as usual. Perhaps they both could have engaged in chit-chat about their holiday but that was not their style. At the end of their liaison, Elizabeth stopped at Damian's table, gazed into his eyes, passed him an envelope, and said, "Oh, dear. I'm sorry," and abruptly left. Damian abruptly opened the note:

Boca Raton for a month

- - -

Sorrow entered Damian's heart, yet a sense of relief entered his mind. His love for Elizabeth had blossomed. He sat and considered the ramifications of love, its irrationality, its mind-altering essence, its pain, its freedoms and constrictions, its sheer foolishness. He was thankful that he finally experienced it, especially without having to talk through it. He felt saved. He was stronger, a better priest, and wondered what it would be like if and when love ended.

The next morning, Mass at Saint Brigid's was sparsely attended, but Elizabeth was there. Damian, in his role as priest, would never use the pulpit to pass a private message. His mind and heart, and Christmas, had been focused on God's forgiving love so it made sense to begin his sermon, "God is love..."

Elizabeth understood and left her final note in the pew:

Powerful

\- - -

Arrival

The bus from New Rochelle to Manhattan delivered commuters to the metropolis every morning and returned them, spent, to their homes every night. Father Xavier Farrell, admitted sinner, sat on the bus, uncomfortable in his clothes, concerned with his luggage, concerned with how to approach his first experience as a parish priest. The Roman collar at his throat made him stick out. Everyone else at least had some color, perhaps a bright hat or a cheerful overcoat for the September weather, green and white for the Jets or blue and white for the Yankees.

Passing Fordham University campus with the tall trees changing color, Xavier recalled his undergraduate days. His memories of academic rigor and social activity were fond, overall. His secrets from Fordham remained, tightly held, in his heart. On the way to his first position as a priest he needed to suppress the past, keep his feelings to himself, and do his duty. *God, shine your grace on me*, he thought.

A businessman spoke up.

"Farrell? Is that you? Fordham, we were in freshman Western Civ together, right?"

"Yes, I'm Farrell. Xavier. Sorry, I don't remember."

Sliding to sit next to Xavier, the man introduced himself in a hushed tone.

"I'm Stanley. Stanley Settler. I thought I recognized you. Wow. They are still making priests?"

"We're not on the endangered species list yet," replied Xavier. "I've wanted to be a priest since first communion."

"Where you headed?"

"Our Lady of Graces. East Ninetieth St. My first parish. Do you know it?"

"Nah. I haven't been to church since Fordham. Is that a confession? Sorry." Once Stanley started talking, he didn't stop. "I'm down at Goldman Sachs. I don't generally take this bus full of stench and baby spit. A driver usually takes me from New Rock City to Goldman. It's so worth it. I'm inches away from resuming my car and driver. One or two big option bets, with somebody else's money, and I'll be golden." His rumpled shirt and overgrown haircut suited his nervous banter. He started to murmur to himself rather than Xavier, tugging on his earlobe. "Won't need to sit on a newspaper to keep my pants from grime. Won't need to eat at Goldman Sachs free canteen. Get work done in the limo. Check my fantasy team. Get the morning business done. Get the MBA paid off, back into a car. Sorry, I'm rambling."

"It's okay. Maybe you should come to Our Lady of Graces sometime."

"Yeah. Maybe. Sometime. I'm pretty busy. Working my way up."

Both embarrassed, they turned their heads to the outside world.

The bus crossed the Third Avenue bridge from the Bronx into Manhattan, making its first stop at 125th Street. Xavier considered the number 125. Genesis 1:25, "God made every kind of wild animal, every kind of tame animal, and every kind of thing that crawls on the ground. God saw that it was good." As they passed through Harlem, he read the signs on the buildings. Free clinic. Get a new phone plan. Easy Divorce, Call Mann & Mann. Shadows of buildings flicked through the bus windows like an old silent movie. The bus flew through synchronized lights down Lexington Avenue. There was a stop near Mount Sinai Medical Center, then the pace slowed as orange cones and barriers protected a tube of steam rising in the middle of a lane. This gave Xavier a chance to prepare to get off the bus.

He moved toward the door with his bags. "Excuse me. 'Scuse me. Thanks, 'Scuse me."

A nearly sleeping man got bumped. "F-off bro. Oh, oh, a priest. Sorry. Sorry, you get a pass. Let me tuck in my feet for you."

"I'm sorry. God bless."

As Xavier climbed off the bus with his roller bag, duffle bag, and briefcase, he was greeted by a sea of activity near the 92Y. The Lexington Avenue sidewalks were full of people, dogs on leashes, newspaper stands, pretzel carts setting up to sell morning coffee, postcard trays, seats for a café, bicycles chained to iron railings. Signs on the outside walls invited people to talks by celebrities, book clubs, AA meetings. Multiple smells shifted in the breeze, floating like leaves in a stream. Some good. Taxis came and went, horns blowing, distant sirens adding to the cacophony of the big city.

Xavier tried to meld into this world. He stepped back from the flow to orient himself. He needed to walk two blocks down Lexington then two blocks east on Ninetieth. He watched the blocks full of humanity. Multiplied by hundreds. Thousands. Millions. Every person seemed to have a direction, a purpose, like bees droning to their duties by instinct. He was an invader to this ordered morning rush. He listened to the hum of the city's motion. A sign flashed the temperature, 51 degrees. Xavier quietly recited Psalm 51, "Have mercy on me God in accord with your merciful love." Near the corner of Lexington Avenue and Ninetieth Street, he saw a pale woman in a dark navy peacoat talking to herself.

Xavier turned toward his new home seeing doormen with caps, metal diamond tread doors recessed in the sidewalk, poles that announced when to park, discarded packing materials, unwanted furniture. The bank sign on Third Avenue flashed 7:51. John 7:51. Something like, "Is it legal to convict a man before he's given a hearing?"

As he walked east down the north side of East Ninetieth Street, the bustle of the avenues was replaced with calmer, Upper East Side residential buildings. It was an easy walk from the bus stop after four years at Fordham, four years of seminary, a year as deacon, a few months at the cathedral. The street was shady with morning sun peeking through the apartment buildings and leafy trees that lined the sidewalks. Some of the fallen leaves accumulated in the gutters. Brick apartment buildings dominated the road, five, six stories high with beautiful doorways but marred by black iron fire escapes.

He reached Ruppert Park on his left-hand side. Across the street loomed Our Lady of Graces, shining in the morning sunlight. The church had an imposing Gothic granite front with wide stairs under a massive stained-glass window. Wrought-iron gates and barriers along the length of the street protected the entrances.

He turned to look through the park, full of green and golden trees. Along the benches, Xavier saw people sitting forward, hands clasped in front of them as if in prayer. He quickly realized they were instead immersed in their personal cell phone spaces. A man approached.

"Can you help the poor, Father? I got mouths to feed."

Xavier saw the condition of the man's clothes and his downtrodden attitude. He dropped his bags and dug into his pocket to provide a few dollars.

"Thanks, man. I mean, father."

"God bless you," Xavier blurted.

"Yeah, gods bless ya too."

Xavier saw a man hurrying out of the church and realized that a Mass was in progress. He carried his luggage up the steps to the entrance, greeted by a lovely statue of Saint Mary with a young Jesus in her arms. The church was stunningly beautiful in the morning light with the high arched stained-glass window prisms spraying gold and sky and rubies onto the pews. Xavier briefly prayed to Our Lady of Graces, asking for her help in his new world. He prayed to her son, asking for forgiveness, guidance, friendship. He stashed his bags on the side of the vestibule and took a seat in the last pew. It was the last moments of Mass. Xavier's eyes were drawn to the front altars with their fine, shining mosaics, five impressive screens, Christ crucified in the center of it all. His new pastor, Monsignor Colin O'Malley, tall, thin, gray, in deep green vestments, gave the final blessing with his fading Irish accent.

Xavier received curious looks from the old church ladies as they passed out of church. The monsignor left the altar and headed to the front of the church, noticing Xavier at the last moment.

"Ah, Father Farrell, no doubt. Well, I need to lock up. You'll have to leave. We have an appointment at 9:15. I will see you then."

Before he could speak, Xavier was shooed out the door, and it was locked behind him. His bags, and his Bible, were locked inside.

Xavier descended the stone stairway and stepped into the street. On Second Avenue, there were small restaurants, a hair salon, a wine bar, an ATM booth, a convenience store, and a laundry service. A block down from the church, a quaint coffee shop attracted his attention. He walked in for a takeout morning coffee and returned to Ruppert Park to wait for his appointment. He approached a convenient bench across from the church and asked a man, "Is anyone sitting here?"

"Just my bag. How you doin'?"

"Good. Good. I'm Father Farrell. Father Xavier. Are you in the parish?"

"Nah. Nah, that a white church. We don't go there. Get a sandwich from it 'bout every Friday though. But, no, don't go there."

"Well, I'm new. Brand-new. But I'm sure everyone is welcome."

After a moment of silence, the two men became relaxed next to each other, both enjoying the morning sun as it penetrated the golden leaves of the park, illuminating the garden floor.

"What's your name?" Xavier asked.

"I'm Tyler."

"Well, Tyler, you are my first new friend in Ruppert Park. It was nice to meet you. I hope to see you around."

"Yeah, you too," Replied Tyler.

Xavier stepped down the granite rectory steps. He pushed the button marked Office and a harsh buzz unlocked the door. He entered a warm vestibule with earthen colored carpets.

"Welcome, Father Farrell. I'm Mrs. Stone. Harriet. The secretary."

Harriet looked about sixty-five years old with short cropped gray hair. She wore a camel hair cardigan sweater over khaki slacks and practical flats. She seemed to be a happy, unstressed person.

"Hello, Harriet. Lovely morning."

"Don't you have any bags?" she asked.

"Ha. Yes, I was a bit early, so I went into the church and the monsignor ushered me out to lock up, so my bags are still up there."

"Oh, you have met Monsignor?"

"Briefly. He said he'd meet me at 9:15 as planned."

"Yes, he will be in then. Would you like a cup of coffee? Tea?"

"Coffee would be nice, thank you, Harriet."

"Let me show you where to get it. The kitchen is just off here."

They stepped through her office to a large pantry that contained tall cabinets, her copier, and a dumb waiter, then continued through to an outdated kitchen. It had wood paneling and maple cabinets.

Harriet said, "On this floor is my office, the kitchen, a small dining room, the formal staircase, then the rest of the floor is the parish hall all the way to the back alley. There is a back staircase and an elevator."

"Well, I'll take a look. Thanks."

Xavier walked through the immaculately clean kitchen and dining room to the parish hall. There were many folded chairs with nowhere to put them, a white board with a child's drawing of a flower and the sun, and the words "God bless us." Boy Scout flags rested next to a flimsy partition. At the end of the long hall, the bathroom was old, worn porcelain from the 1950s.

Xavier's shoes echoed on the wooden planks as he returned to Harriet's office. The dusty windows near the ceiling allowed some morning sunlight into the hall. Xavier noticed the imposing granite church when he looked up through each window as he passed. The gargoyles and spouts peeked into the church hall and the aged, verdigris copper roof produced a pale green glow on the buttresses and Gothic features. Shadows, mixes of light and dark, revealed glimpses of the darkened exterior stained glass.

Arriving back at the kitchen the scent of fresh coffee dominated. Harriet had set up a silver tray of two porcelain cups with saucers, a small pitcher of cream, a silver sugar bowl, and a plastic carafe of steaming coffee. She placed the tray on the dumb waiter and sent it up one flight. Xavier followed Harriet up the formal staircase to the reception hall of the parish pastor. Xavier noticed the richly carved balustrade and elegant sitting room furniture outside the front office, distinctly contrasting with the rather aged parish facilities below. The area provided a lovely, warm feeling, good for impressing people, donors and such, Xavier thought.

"I'll see if Monsignor is ready for you." She knocked and entered the office.

From outside, Xavier saw the monsignor raise his arm to stop Harriet.

"I need to return a call from the cardinal," he said. "The child priest will have to wait out there for a bit."

Xavier could not help overhearing the words. He turned his attention to pictures of baby Jesus with Mary, the pope, and Patrick Cardinal Brophy.

Harriet interrupted his thoughts, "Monsignor is on the phone, please have a seat, Father." She retreated to her office. Xavier waited, well past his appointment time. At 9:40, he descended to Harriet's desk to ask her what to do.

"Maybe it was a test to see how patient you would be. Go to his door and knock, then enter. Even if he is still on the phone, he may wave you in."

Xavier did as instructed. In Monsignor Colin O'Malley's office, the old priest was staring through the front Gothic arched windows at the park across the street. The office was decorated sparingly. The blonde maple paneling and shelving complemented the deep red Persian carpet. Shelves were stuffed with books spilling over in stacks on the floor, desk, and coffee table. An art deco lamp on the desk gave tinted light along with sunshine filtering through stained glass. Still gazing across the street, the monsignor finally spoke.

"When I first arrived, fourteen years ago, the park was filled with mothers and children playing on the swings and slides. Now, if there is a child there, a foreign housekeeper or maid or Asian babysitter sits on a bench staring at a cell phone, barely watching. Vagrants take over the benches. Piss wherever, stink the place up. This church is an oasis of peace and calm. Do you understand?"

"I think I do."

"Have a seat." Xavier perceived this more as an order than an offer. "Welcome, Xavier, to the parish. I am Monsignor O'Malley. I am so very grateful that this parish can maintain two priests. Of course, you can be helpful, even though you have much to learn from my tutelage."

The monsignor's eyes were kind and his speech measured with a slight, warm brogue, but some of the words were firm. Xavier felt perplexed by this dichotomy.

"I want you to know, this is my parish. I have been here over fourteen years. I know every inch of it, I know every person who matters. Someday, maybe you too can call it yours. But for now, I set out the rules and you follow them."

"Of course, Monsignor."

"The previous young man did not understand this so I must be quite clear with you. The church has a foundation of truth. Father Dickerson's new ideas didn't work. Poor little Jason, God be with him. He so wanted to miraculously receive the wounds of Christ. No stigmata for him."

After a moment of consideration, Monsignor O'Malley continued abruptly.

"Your time off will be Tuesday evening until Thursday morning. I require that you leave, go somewhere else. This is for your own good, believe me. Be back to serve the 7:30 a.m. Mass. I leave Thursday when my duties are done and return Saturday morning. Any questions?"

"No. I understand."

"As this is your first day and you will need to set up your room and office, you can stay here this week. Harriet will fill in details of your schedule. Follow my rules, which of course are the rules of the church. I think you will make no waves here. There is no need to make waves. No need. We will get along. We live in the same house, we'll see each other around the place, of course, but I also want to meet formally every week to discuss your progress."

"Thank you, Monsignor."

"Thank you. Oh, wait, let's pray for you and our parish." After a brief, silent pause, he continued. "Now you are dismissed."

Xavier did not feel like they had just prayed, but he did feel like he was dismissed so he stood up and walked out, quite bewildered.

Golden Blood

When his last run was over, and the commuter train sat on the tracks at the end of the Red Line in Braintree, Dwayne walked from front to back to pick up the trash and make sure the train was empty. He made quick work of it until he reached the last car. It's always the last car. A soft covered book, left behind, lay on the floor, under a seat, tucked in the crumpled fold of today's *Boston Herald*. Dwayne picked it up and was about to toss it into his trash bag, but he decided to take a look. It was somebody's handwritten journal, no name anywhere. The first page of the journal read: "March 3rd. This sucks. This sucks. This sucks. This sucks." On and on it went.

Dwayne sat down and leafed through the pages. Some were filled with: "Rh null, Rh-null, Rh-Null" over and over. Other full pages of "Not paranoid, not paranoia, not paranoid" and "They watch me, they watch me, they watch me" and "Golden blood. Golden blood. Golden blood." This sucks and other full pages evolved to more elegant writing, more details, more intrigue.

Dwayne flipped to a page of writing near the Golden Blood rant.

> March 11th: Having Rh-null blood (who would even know?), somehow makes me special? They call it golden blood. I don't get what's so special. Okay, there are only a few people worldwide with Rh-null blood. So what? I say blood inside body—good, blood outside body—not so good, try to keep blood in body. I don't have any antigens. Golden blood. Seems more of a burden. They want my blood every month. Universal donor but Rh-nulls can only get the golden blood. There's a stash I just replenished for myself at Rhode Island Hospital. Woopie. You know who also wants it. Them. The watchers. I'm not kidding. That's why I'm not paranoid. Somebody keeps an eye on me. Flies. 8,000 eyes.

> Somebody not from here. Flies. Flies are watching me. Always travel in pairs. Maybe they are alien fly drones. I don't know but I act like I don't notice them. Never tell anybody. Not even Doc Ambrose. God, I sound crazy. How do you prove yourself not paranoid? Just don't tell anybody. Find out the symptoms and then don't show the symptoms. Swat the flies. Kill the flies.

Dwayne flipped to today:

> Here I go again, up to Boston. It's kind of a pain, every other Tuesday, especially when it was raining like today, driving up from Providence, parking at Quincy Adams, and taking the Red Line to South Station, but if any of my family knew my real secret. I don't know. Maybe there should be an Rh-Null support group. Are they being watched too? Maybe I should tell Stephie. Maybe she would understand. No. I can't. I'll just

keep talking to Doc Ambrose. I can trust her. She doesn't believe me so that's good. I tell her good stories. I can't tell her that the two flies in her window really aren't flies. She would just think I'm paranoid. And crazy. Today I told her about my friend from school who said she was an alien. Doc knows I am wasting time until we get to the real reason I see her. She knows. I know. Same old prescription—relaxation techniques.

Okay, okay, I am crazy. Not paranoid. It would only be paranoid if I was imagining and irrational. I really am the 'subject of persistent, intrusive behavior by others.' I'm not imagining it. The flies. Alien flies *are* after me. They are after my golden blood. They are following me back to South Station. I don't see them right now, but they will show up on the T.

I choose the second car, heading back to Quincy Adams. Not too many people on the train. No flies so far. But. But. But. OMG, I just met eyes with the most beautiful woman I've ever seen. Her dark, emerald eyes looked right through me, pierced into me. I didn't mean to meet her eyes. Now, I can't look back at her. But I have to. Quick, sly peek. OMG, she's still piercing me. Beauty. Mid to late twenties maybe. Auburn hair to her shoulders, dark eyes, a fine Burberry raincoat. Quick look again. She is staring out the window. Okay, okay. Relief. But now I can't stop peeking. I have a great need to say something. No. no. I feel like I love her. No. Crazy. Her dark red lipstick has pressed a half kiss onto the Starbucks cup rim. Fly lands on the outer edge of her cup. She gently waves it away. Oh. I see. Is she with the flies? Maybe. The wave was way too gentle. Her smart phone rings, and she speaks. Yes, this is Aurora. Today? Yes, today would be perfect.

I'm nervous. But I'm going to say it and get off the train. Here comes the UMass-JFK stop.

Dwayne, even though he would be late for dinner, couldn't stop reading.

> I let two trains pass and got back on, last car, empty. Creature. Why did I say that to her? She has probably already been told that she's the most beautiful creature on earth. Why did I say creature? OMG. I thought she was just going to stare. But. But. But. Why did she look right into my eyes, smile, and say, "Thank you, nice to meet you, this is your day." And why did she tell me not to worry? What does it mean? It's crazy, paranoid, to think maybe this was going to be the day she and the flies would finally take me. To whatever planet or spaceship or something. They want my golden blood, my Rh-null, to evaluate it, or something.
>
> North Quincy station. Still alone.
>
> Wollaston station. Doors open, doors close. I don't know why, but my heart is pounding. Am I just making myself crazy? I crumple my

> *Boston Herald* and search for flies. I see none. Just have Quincy Center, then the next stop to get off, get to my car.
>
> Quincy Center, doors open. Two flies in, two more flies, Aurora…

The old train conductor looked around the empty car and pondered the incomplete entry. He saw nothing else, no signs of struggle, no signs at all. Dwayne decided to take the mysterious journal home to show to his wife.

Two flies made their way to the train's driving compartment to await further orders.

In Plain Sight

The majesty of Grand Central Station made an impression on people. Tourists looked up in awe to see the aqua-blue firmament of celestial constellations. Janitors felt the immensity of the constant need to sweep up behind the flow of shuffling feet. Commuters experienced a vast outdoor openness as they emerged from their underground caves. Lovers felt the romance of twinkling lights, and the intimate privacy of being together even as the exciting buzz of humanity floated by, completely ignoring their canoodling.

Jimmy and Nancy also felt mostly ignored and unnoticed as they blended in with the tourists and commuters, looking for leftover scraps. This was a good place to pick up an unfinished pretzel or anything that might help them survive. They talked about getting a place in the country, maybe heading to Florida in the winter.

Jimmy said, "I'm willing to go anywhere that's not here, but maybe anywhere except up where your momma lives. Providence is not my idea of pleasant living." Nancy just smiled. As she took her perch near the Metro North ticket counter, she politely pointed out that things would have to wait as there was a bun in the oven, almost ready. Jimmy, ever vigilant and protective, lovingly pecked her on the forehead, then resumed his patrol. He followed along with the commuter traffic to the far end of the hall, looking for the right opportunity.

Suddenly, Nancy called out, "Jimmy, Jimmy, Jimmy! Come quick!" Jimmy flew to her, avoiding the authorities and mass of humanity, arriving just in time, above the Metro North ticket counter, to see his newborn chick break free from its shell and begin chirping in their nest.

Electra

I was so stressed out by trying to keep them apart physically and emotionally, I needed a fresh start. She knew I was married but insisted that she wanted the thrill of having a place near me so she could visit my Yorkville, meet in my familiar places, cause excitement, court the danger of being caught. She wanted a sugar daddy paying for a pied-à-terre in Manhattan. In no way did I want her anywhere near my home. I couldn't handle that. Elizabeth wouldn't handle that. I convinced myself breaking up like a pair of teens or ghosting her was not enough. Stacey had to no longer exist.

The end started in Stacey's city, Seattle, during one of my frequent, sometimes manufactured, business trips. After meeting with the Microsoft team, I had a free day to ferry over to Bainbridge Island and drive to Olympic National Park. Taking the ferry across Puget Sound in the dawn mist was calming and prepared me for my mycology quest. I was surprised by how incredibly calm I was. I felt like I was in a hypnotic state, a robot carrying out a command that someone else had given me, expressionless, cold-hearted. I didn't see it through my own eyes. I saw it like I was a drone hovering over myself, recording the action.

In Olympic, I found a trail that led through a moss-shrouded hemlock forest. It soon transitioned to a stately old-growth oak stand. No one was around. The only sound was far off wind blowing, making a rushing, hissing sound through the forest. Near the hardened path, where the sun trickled slightly through the overhead canopy, a multitude of mushrooms sprouted in the undergrowth. The damp floor smelled of wonderfully pungent fertility and tasty fungi. I identified shiitake and hedgehog, then finally my prize, *Amanita phalloides*, the death cap. When young, it is a beautiful little olive green and pale white button with a musty, irresistible scent and a firm cap. You expect fairies to be nearby with these little beauties. They say it tastes great and makes you want more. The few people who survive this killer say that. Using a plastic bag for a mitten, I quickly but carefully picked six death caps from the base of a giant oak, slipping them into a bag. I thanked the oak like it was a Manhattan haberdasher providing the perfectly matched button. "Good day, sir."

I slipped back to the hardened path only to encounter a millennial National Park Ranger, annoyed that I had left the man-made trail and trampled on the pristine forest floor. Her khaki uniform shirt with dark green pants were immaculately groomed, and she would have presented a classic ranger look except for the muffin-top bulge at her waistline. To me, it looked like a tan mushroom cap hanging over a green tuft of grass. She looked me up and down.

"It is illegal to remove anything but memories from a national park. It is rude to leave the designated trail. What were you doing?"

Before I could answer, she continued, "If everyone trampled just anywhere, the ecosystem would be even more damaged beyond what humans have already inflicted. Stay on the trails or stay out of the park. You get me? Were you taking a selfie?"

Again, she did not give me time to answer. "And do not tell me that you were pissing in the woods. That would not be good. You would be interrupting nature. Well, the real nature. Not human nature."

Finally, I was able to speak, "Officer, sorry. Yes, I was taking a selfie in the streams of sunlight. Sorry. I'll be leaving now. Staying on the trail. No worries. Sorry. I'm heading back to New York."

I am not a violent person, and Ranger Regina was not wrong, but in my robotic scheme to use these poison mushrooms to kill, I briefly thought about jamming some death caps down her throat. But then, more shrooms would be needed for my intended purposes, and I was not supposed to leave the trail, so I headed back to Seattle. From the stern of the ferry, the Olympic mountains loomed. They were aptly named. Zeus, Aphrodite, and Hades would be at home up there. I gave a pet name to the poisonous friend in my pocket—Electra, a nymph of Zeus.

I returned to Seattle and went to Pike Place Market, bought a quart of mushroom soup from a farmer's stand, along with the last flowers I would ever give to Stacey. I grabbed a fresh baguette and a fine bottle of Napa Valley Merlot. Stacey and I had plans to meet in her apartment around six after she got out of work. Before then, I met with some of the Microsoft crowd for a drink with Electra in my jacket, patiently waiting to do her thing. After one pint, I had an urge to show her to my colleagues. After the second pint, I wanted to take a small taste of Electra. Instead, I searched the bar, half expecting Stacey to be hiding out with some other boyfriend. I didn't need for her to be the evil one. One evil was enough. I didn't need liquid courage to go through with my plan, but Bushmills twenty-one-year-old single malt caught my eye in the mirrored bar shelf.

The nectar of the gods. My friends and I toasted to health, to love, to the gods. I departed.

I went to her apartment early, using the key she had given me a year ago, when we both thought the affair was working.

I opened the wine bottle to let the merlot breath, opened the plastic bag to let Electra breath. I poured some of the untainted soup into a bowl, then dumped it out, leaving the empty bowl with some residue of the soup as a prop to show I ate some. I carefully chopped half the death cap mushrooms into the soup for Stacey. I spoke to Electra as I chopped, told her she and Stacey would mix, they would love each other. My other death caps were returned to the plastic bag for possible future use back in New York. One never knows when a few death caps might come in handy. Then I poured myself some wine, ate some of the bread, turned the stove on to warm the soup, waited impatiently for my soon-to-be poisoned ex-girlfriend to get home. I thought about what would happen. Symptoms of poisoning wouldn't show up until long after I was on my return flight. She would get a stomachache in the night, try to ignore it. By the next morning, it would be too late for effective treatment. She would vomit a bit. Then violently. Her liver and kidneys would be attacked by the toxins, cutting off protein synthesis, causing cell death, major organ failure.

My own dulled, slurred, robotic mind wouldn't have to watch it happen.

Stacey arrived home later than expected, which fit right into my plan. She paused to provide a nearly collegial kiss, the sad result of a dying relationship. No longer did she tilt her head partially to the side, bobbing her auburn hair off one shoulder. She didn't close her eyes slightly or open her lips a little, anticipating a passionate embrace. She didn't reach her arms up to my shoulders or caress the back of my neck with her fingernails. No matter, it convinced me that I was not the only one who knew it was over. I tried to perk up and get her to take the plunge.

"I had a few drinks with Morgan and the guys, got over here pissed and hungry, so I started without you, babe. Sorry. I nearly ate all the bread. It's good. Here you go. This mushroom soup is unbelievable."

She kicked off her spike heels, flopped onto the kitchen counter chair, and said, "Yeah, hon. Looks like you have had a few drinks. Let me catch up a little. It was a long, hard day."

"Of course. Yeah, relax. Here's a nice merlot. Plenty left for you. There was brie in the fridge. Here you go. Nice with the baguette too. You really have to try this soup. It's warm, out of this world, to die for."

I didn't want to oversell her poisonous bowl, but it needed to go down her throat. I ladled an ample portion and placed it in front of her on the counter. I robotically stared into her beautifully dark hazel eyes for the last time. "I'm going to miss you. Sorry."

"Wait, what? I thought you were staying tonight."

"No, ah, babe, I'm taking the red eye back. I have to leave pretty soon. I have an important, ah, meeting to get back to in New York."

"Oh, Raymond. Okay."

No begging me to stay. No wishing I would stay. Just plain old love fatigue. Finally, the first spoonful of Electra and her soupy companions entered Stacey's mouth and I felt better. I watched her enjoy the death cap soup. I had an urge to taste it. I enjoyed watching her progress toward our breakup.

"Oh, this soup is gorgeous. Thanks."

"You're welcome. To your health." In my buzzed state, I raised my glass of wine and saluted. I stood in the kitchen watching her, staring at her, silently coaxing her to relax and take in the remainder of her fateful broth. I thought she had consumed enough to do the trick.

But then I thought about the next morning, after I was long gone. I didn't think about her. I thought about my fingerprints. The plastic container from Pikes Place. I turned away from her, saw the sink, the stovetop, the saucepans, and utensils. How could I hide all the fingerprints that were everywhere throughout her apartment? I couldn't. I blurted, "Oh god. I'm sorry."

"What is it?"

"I need to get outta here. I mean, let me clean up a little, then I have to drive down to Sea-Tac, turn in the rental, and get the red eye. Sorry, sorry."

Resignedly, Stacey said, "You don't need to clean anything. If you need to go, just go."

At that point, she was right. Everything was mechanically in place to happen. "Que sera, sera. Whatever will be, will be."

Our parting was not like it used to be when we couldn't keep our hands off each other. It was a sad nothingness. A dull duty. I felt an absurd down-hearted melancholy. I knew she felt it too. I knew she would die, but I thought she knew something was off too. I don't think she cared about my ability to drive with a buzz on. That wasn't it. Woman's intuition, so damn bothersome. In weakness, I said, "Don't be afraid. I will be back in a few weeks. On the first."

My robotic self took over for the drive to the airport and check-in for the flight. I hardly remember the dull space between her apartment and my seat on the plane. While the death cap toxins began to hurt her, somewhere up in the darkness of flyover country, I entered the tiny lavatory at the back of Delta Flight 970. I stared at myself in the mirror, robot eyes looking back at robot eyes. What had they done? They executed the plan. How many times had I said sorry without meaning it? Electra, my death cap, my new love, led the way. I took the shrooms out of my pocket, opened the plastic bag. I breathed in her moist, delicate, musty fragrance. So tempting to taste. So tempting to eat.

The plane rattled as it passed through an unseen turbulence of the gods and the ding of the Return to Your Seat light popped. I stayed, staring at myself. I thought of the future investigation. I didn't do everything right. I was too simpleminded about the whole thing. I did nothing right. She would die, but somebody would try to figure out how. Fingerprints. That farmer's stand. Should I have taken the plastic container and tossed it away at the airport? Will anyone think murder? Or was it just an accident? Should I have stayed and watched it happen, then clean up evidence of myself? Oh my god, her cellphone. I meant to steal that. I might be all over it. Surveillance videos. They are everywhere now. Witnesses, Ranger Regina in Olympic Park, the Asian lady who sold me the flowers, the soup man. He will be pissed about being accused. Two wine glasses. She had a visitor. A killer.

The plane bounced hardily through the turbulent skies. Zeus was active in the skies over Olympus.

The flight attendant knocked on my door. "Sir, you have to return to your seat. Is everything okay in there?" I didn't respond. My new friend Electra rested on the tiny sink counter in front of me, tempting me, waiting.

Horsepower

We trotted side by side. Lilith loved horses, and I loved to be by her side.

"Do you think we will own our own horses some day?"

There was only one acceptable answer, but I was afraid to give it. What was she really asking? She was imagining a future with me. She was thinking about a courtship, a wedding, a marriage. I was supposed to start that from my knee at a romantic dinner, not from horseback.

I gave my Palomino a kick. He broke into a gallop as I fearfully yelled over my shoulder, "If you can catch me!"

Sunday Down City

Young Father James went where the September wind led him. The breeze pushed him toward the east from Saint Peter and Paul Cathedral toward the Providence River. He was surprised by the peacefulness of Sunday in the city. The streets were quieter, the traffic diminished. The staccato weekdays were replaced by a smoother, legato weekend. On the sidewalks, he observed more casual speeds with college students strolling along Weybosset Street for pleasure. The vibrant colors of the street near Providence Performing Arts Center seemed to mute into softer pastels. Still, the ever-present vagrants roamed their territories, nearly invisible to others unless they cared to look.

He had been to the river park before, but this time, as a resident, he looked at it with new eyes. He solemnly walked through the Remembrance Garden with the multitude of engraved path stones commemorating the loss of children. He paused to look at names, to lament the losses people had to endure. A little further down river, the riverfront 195 District Park was a quiet green space, providing a nature-filled sanctuary for the weary. Rhode Islanders and visitors took advantage of the open lawns, river views, and hidden gardens. James walked the paths to plan a route to run in the mornings. He was determined to maintain a habit he had developed in high school—to run and pray. He crossed the modern wooden foot bridge and paused in the middle of the river. He observed the down city skyline to the north and west, and the river leading into the Narragansett Bay to the south. His heart swelled as he envisioned a safe place to escape from the cathedral when needed. As he walked along the east side of the river walk, he noticed turtles sunning themselves at the water's edge. He said, "I'll see you two tomorrow morning. My goal is to see you at least four times a week." He laughed at himself for talking to the animals like Saint Francis would.

James wore a red plaid shirt to try to imitate a layperson, but his black trousers and black shoes, and perhaps his demeanor, didn't hide his identity. It was cool, with autumn colors clinging to wiry branches. The fresh petrichor scent of recent rain and the crunchy leaves underfoot helped block out the less pleasant aspects of city living. He found an unoccupied, dry bench, and opened his prayer book. Before he could finish one prayer, an intruder into his personal sanctuary arrived to share his seat. A plump gray squirrel, accustomed to human handouts, gave a cautious flit of his head and a wave with his bushy gray tail.

"Go away," James said, but his voice was too kind, and the creature moved a little closer. James had no treat to provide, but he remembered he had the power of absolution. "Your sins are forgiven, rodent." The animal scampered away happy, free. With a light chuckle, James thought about how easy and accepting the creature was. If only people could be so open-minded, without a care in the world. The squirrel had no deep philosophical contemplation, just easy acceptance.

James stood and again walked with the breeze along Providence River Walk. He heard a voice from the ground on the eastern edge of the path, near Point Street bridge, "Hey, hey, I know you. I saw you in church."

"Oh, hello. I'm James. I don't remember seeing you, sorry."

"Well, I know who you are. You new. New. What do you do?

"I'm a priest. I talk to people. Sometimes it helps. Do you want to talk?" James squatted down near the dark man. He noticed well-worn sneakers, clean white socks, at least four layers of clothes, gray stubble against dark brown skin, and a heavy-duty plastic bag twisted closed, bunched up next to the man.

"I am talking. Am talking."

"I'm Father James. What's your name?"

"My name? You want to know my name? Nobody. Nobody wants to know my name. We gave our names away."

"No. You didn't. Who told you that?" James moved closer, sitting on a piece of his new friend's cardboard.

"That's my. That's my patio. You can sit there."

"Thank you."

They sat, James peacefully, sensing the other man was less sure if he wanted anyone to encroach on his domain. A couple passed by on the river walk, perhaps curious about the black and white differences of the odd couple of men sitting together in the sun. Two pigeons scampered up, seeking to join this new fellowship just for crumbs. James thought of the two men who met the resurrected Jesus on the road to Emmaus.

James finally spoke up.

"That pigeon's name is Cleopus. Well, my friend, I suppose I should be on my way. Have a…"

"It's Benny!" the man blurted urgently. "My name is Benny."

"Okay, Benny. I'm pleased to meet you. I have to leave soon. I'm heading to visit Saint Joseph's on Hope Street."

"You can stay," Benny said as he crabbed over to provide a foot more space on the cardboard. "Here. Here, come into my parlor. Please. Please." James shuffled over closer to Benny. "Tuesdays. I, I go to Joseph's on Tuesdays. They have soup. Tuesday."

An older man in a woolly cardigan bent over and placed a dollar in Benny's worn Dunkin' Donuts cup.

"Thank you, sir," they said together.

James added, "God bless you."

"Benny, do you go to the Beneficent Church for coffee on Friday mornings? Maybe I will see you there."

"Yes, yes, I do. Sometimes. Usually. Good coffee. William is nice. Nice."

"Well, maybe I will see you there. I try to go every Friday."

"That's right. Maybe. You know William? He's nice. Girl is nice too. Nice. I try to come up on Friday morning. I try."

The autumn breeze softly ruffled Benny's cardboard. He was pleased. Before James stood to leave, he looked into Benny's eyes, and reached out his hand. "Benny, it was nice to meet you. Thanks for inviting me to sit down. Peace be with you."

"I didn't want you to sit. Didn't. But now I'm glad you did. I'll see you. See you."

Mariam

Climbing onto the T at Longwood, an unkempt man yanked his woman as she clumsily lifted her baby. He scowled and nudged them to the rear.

His shouting aroused the car's attention. Most people turned away. Mariam's baby, at the front of the car, did not. He kicked at Mariam's ribcage, coaxing her to action.

Mariam walked back, asking for pardon as she passed. Utterly ignoring the irate man, Mariam seized the crying baby, cradling him next to her son. She lovingly took the mother by her elbow, escorting her forward as the sea of commuters closed the path behind them.

Absolution

As he unfolded out of bed, going directly onto his bare knees, Father Xavier gazed at the subtle crimson and golden light that began to seep through the arched stained glass of his chamber. He usually woke before sunrise in the gloomy, rising, encouraging dawn. He paused, cleared his mind as best he could, and began the morning as he had every morning since he was ordained nearly a year ago: "God, come to my assistance. Lord, make haste to help me." It was the beginning of the divine office, a series of prayers spread throughout the day Catholic priests and religious were required to pray every day.

Xavier finished lauds and continued his morning routine. It was never routine. Something always surprised or diverted him. This chilly spring morning was no different. He expected to take his morning stroll, say Mass at seven thirty, then have a light breakfast before office hours, or a funeral, or a hospital call, or a family home crisis visit. Before departing, he investigated the mirror and saw a young man, untroubled. He also glimpsed the future man, worn, depleted, stained like the inflamed glass, aged. He stepped out of Our Lady of Graces' sturdy gothic rectory on the south side of East Ninetieth Street into an icy mist. A few bundled up commuters rushed along the sidewalk like drones doing their instinctual duties. Bunched at his doorstep in a swaddling pile of stinking wet wool blankets laid a human form. A grubby head peeked out from the reeking blankets and a body began to stretch from an uncomfortable slumber.

Father Xavier paused on the step above the fluctuating, grumbling, and pungent hulk. He stepped over the bundle and bent down to confront the gritty man. Xavier wanted to say, "Why are you here?" but he knew the answer. He peered directly into the bloodshot eyes. There he noticed piercing, cloudy sky-blue eyes like his own. The two men stared at each other, perhaps both challenging each other's will to turn away. The standoff provided Xavier a moment to contemplate his life, his vocation, his mission. His response was "What's your name?"

Shocked at not being immediately expelled from his crib, the vagrant managed to grumble, "Sorry. Percy."

"Percy, I absolve you from your sins in the name of the Father and of the Son and of the Holy Spirit. Your sins are forgiven. Go and sin no more. God bless you."

Xavier shocked himself. He immediately straightened and briskly stepped away, disappearing, escaping, toward Third Avenue. His morning walk was shrouded in a shimmering, misty September dawn. A few bundled-up commuters rushed along the sidewalk. Xavier was stunned. He did that to Percy without thinking. He was not supposed to say those words of sacramental absolution without following detailed church rules, such as allowing the penitent to reveal his sins out loud, resolving to sin no more, and assigning a penance. But he had done it. *What would it mean? How much harm could it do?*

Percy too was stunned. He did not know what to do.

What did he mean? Sins? Forgiven? Just last night's? My mistakes don't matter anymore? Is my entire life clean? Am I clean? Washed? Absolved? Who was that? A priest? What now? Where do I go? What do I do? Do I really have a fresh start?

Needing to find answers, Percy gathered up all his belongings, wrapped his army surplus blanket over his shoulder, and tucked it into his oversized belt and galloped in the direction the priest had gone. He followed in the direction the priest had headed but found nothing. The morning sun warmed his path, scattering the mist. At Fifth Avenue, a police officer near the Church of the Heavenly Rest eyed him suspiciously. It was unlikely the Catholic priest would be inside there, so Percy felt perplexed. But he was free. What was he chasing? He turned and slowly wandered. On the way, he ran into a neighbor, a fellow scrapper in the trade, Carol, pushing her shopping cart laden with nothingness.

"Hey, where you go?" she muttered. "That ain't your direction. Ain't you uselly in Rupe-pit Park? Or at Mister Wright's?"

"Carol. Carol, I'm looking for a man."

"So am I, Sugar."

"No, no. I mean a priest. He forgave me. He freed me. Where did he go? I don't know what to do now."

Carol shrugged and resumed her morning shopping among discarded refuse and street droppings. At that moment, Percy noticed the meager belongings in Carol's cart. He looked directly into her eyes. As usual, she turned her face away. Percy lifted a wry, perceptive smile. He unstrapped his prized blanket from his shoulder, folded it neatly and softly placed it in the cart. He touched Carol on the shoulder then calmly walked back toward Ruppert Park and Our Lady of Graces.

Percy entered the church to a cacophony of old hens clucking: "Where is Father Xavier?" "He's fifteen minutes late for Mass." "There's no answer at the rectory door." "Is Mass cancelled?" "No Mass?" No one knew what to do without a priest. From the rear of the church, Percy blocked out the noise like any city dweller could, saw past the old parishioners, saw the majesty of the altar with brilliant red and golden light streaming through the tall gothic windows. He sat in the back row and pondered his new situation. A memory from his childhood churchgoing emerged: "Speak, Lord, your servant is listening." He noticed a lovely blue image of the Lady of Graces whispering to a youthful child Jesus. Percy closed his eyes, cleared his mind as best he could, and in his heart raised a new prayer to heaven: "God, please help me. I need you as soon as possible." A child's teardrop wept from his eye.

He stood, stepped outside to face the city, the park, the north wind, and decided it was time to visit his mother.

One Messed-Up Sinner

"Hey, Father Damian, belly up to the bar. Stanley, the usual for my favorite priest. Jameson's, one rock."

As I moved my stool over to give big Damian a little more room, I was glad he showed up because I had a question: "Father, are dreams sins? What happens when we sleep? I had an odd dream, woke up feeling like I had sinned."

"No, Charles. Not exactly. You're no sinner. Trust me. You're about the most sinless person I know. I think dreams coax your mind to sort out experience, feelings, stuff like that."

"Hmph. Well, maybe you don't know me as well as you think. The nightmare I had last night was chilling. I was in a church, your church actually, and for some reason I was up front, instead of in my normal back row, conducting a ceremony. Twenty or so women were sitting in the front pews, and I was on a raised platform with a single kneeler in front of me. Behind me and behind the altar table was a long halberd, a spear with twin headed blades. The blades were as big as an elephant's head and the shaft and blades formed the shape of a cross. The tinted light from the stained glass gleamed off the blade edges.

"I looked up to your beautiful pale blue ceiling with the gothic rib vaults. The ribs seemed to transform into thick snakes and elephant trunks as well as alligator backs and elephant legs. The pale blue transformed to tropical green. All the outside light was blotted out by the seething mass of animals and foliage. The congregation sat perfectly still as we were plunged into jungle darkness.

"An acolyte, perhaps twenty years old, tall and thin, lit two torches in each transept, left and right, and they flickered, undulating red and yellow light. I opened an ancient looking book and read a name: 'Allison Finch.' An intake of air from all the women expressed a surprise. Up stood Allison. Perhaps the youngest person in the crowd, just a young adult among the mostly elderly group, she confidently and gracefully strutted up the aisle. Her short red hair bobbed as she happily, innocently approached the kneeler.

"'Are you prepared?' I asked.

"'I am.'

"'You are so young, my child.'

"'I am, but I am ready to give everything, no matter what.'

"'So be it,' I stammered.

"Young, innocent Allison raised her arms, and the similarly aged acolyte draped a white church robe over her head, onto her shoulders. Two incense burners near Allison were stoked and provided sweet, exotic scent to the atmosphere. The smoke of incense rose to the pulsating vault and the torch lights provided an eerie sense of doom.

"Allison removed her shoes and knelt. The empty marble altar and the crucifix transformed into molten lava."

Damian interrupted, "Sounds odd, Charles, but crazy, not sinful. Maybe it depends what you will do to this girl. Who is she, someone you know?"

"I don't think so, there is only one red head in my life, and she is only on the periphery, the art intern at Sotheby's.

"Here is the weirdest part of the dream. All the jungle and the flames and smoke made it seem, instead, that we were inside the mouth, or lungs, or some inside part of a beast. We seemed to be in a breathing, heart pumping, undulating living thing.

"The young altar boy took the halberd from its stand and began to rotate the blades like they were an airplane propeller. He moved around the altar and shifted the blades to a horizontal plane above his head. While Allison kneeled before me, my hands placed on her soft, silky veil of hair, the torches and smoke, and jungle-like beast closing in around us, the halberd found its intended mark. My head was lopped off and crimson blood from my neck pulsated out, showering Allison. I awoke abruptly, dead, tired, scared."

"Wow. Yes, Charles, you are one messed-up sinner."

"Yeah, Father, that is what I thought."

Bertrand Olive Duggan
Letter to Father Woods

Bertrand Olive Duggan
Prisoner 44089B
New Hampshire State Prison for Men
281 North State St.
Concord, NH 03302

Father James Woods
Saint Charles Borromeo
Route 25
Meredith, NH

Dear Father Woods,

I met you at Breebrook prison a few years ago. Maybe you don't remember me, but I remember you. Maybe it was more than just a few years ago. Well, here I am in jail again, this time I'm on death row. There are only two of us in the whole state of New Hampshire. The other guy I ain't met yet, but he has had some cruel and unusual punishment. He's been waiting over ten years for them to kill him. The New Hampshire legislature voted to abolish the death penalty, so maybe he had some hope. Then the governor veto it. That is pretty bad.

I'm in solitary, waiting. They don't call it solitary, but that's what it is. They bring food to me. I get to walk out in the yard, but only when no one else is out there. Not even Wally. That's the other guy they are going to kill. But they don't even have a gallows or electric chair or gas chamber. They say its gonna take 2 million dollars to make. I ain't worth 2 mil. They should just set me in with the others. A shiv will take me out for free. Save lots of taxes.

Everyone hates me. The other inmates yell from the windows, through the bars. They scream baby killer. Twin killer. Die, pig. Other disgusting things. It used to bother me, but now I walk out to the wall and stay out there. When I go out to walk, they used to keep me in cuffs and chains. It was cruel. I'm not going anywhere. They don't need to be that cruel.

I know I am a bad person. My ex won't come see me no more. My mother don't come no more. She came every month, but now she's dead. Those bastards—sorry, Father, but there ain't no other word for them. Well, maybe one or two worse ones. They didn't let me go to the funeral. She didn't show up for a visit. She was already in the ground when they told me. She died April 12. They told me like April 20. Bastards. That was last year. I wasn't even convicted yet. I was still innocent until proven guilty, and then they didn't even prove me guilty. They just reasonably doubted I done it. That ain't no justice. I told them I didn't kill Trudy or the twins. They was just only like three-year-olds. But I was there, then Roger, the husband, came home. I self-defensed myself. He done the others. My DNA was everywhere coz Trudy and me did it in lots of places all over that trailer. Roger and me fighting musta knocked over a ashtray or something. That's why it burned down. I didn't start no fire like the lawyers said. They was dead already but not by my hand. It was definitely Roger. They burned together as a family. And the other trailer had two old people just about dead anyway. They were unintended consequences. I think they took advantage and just lit their own fire to finish their own lives together. They could of got up and got out, but they didn't want to. Then my court appointed lawyer told me to shut my trap. He was right. I was trapped. I should have told them nothing, let them figure it out.

I try to learn to pray, but all I got is this confusing Bible. There is a lot of killing in this Bible. Whole tribes wiped out. No wonder they finally had to say, "Thou shalt not kill" anymore. They coulda wiped out the whole human race. All the killing. And I don't read too good. I can read or write. I ain't no fool. I'm writing this to you right now. But I lose focus. Books can be so boring. And too long too. If I could watch TV, I could do that all day. I used to like the home fixing-up shows. These bastards don't let me have a TV. I see a cable hookup near the floor in my cell. They could give me a TV. I can sometimes hear the guards' TV in the control room when it is quiet all over, everywhere. I sometimes get a ten-second glimpse as I go by on my fifty-minute walk twice a day. I never seen the Patriots win a Superbowl. I was always in jail. Except I was in medium security in 2008 and 2012, but they lost both.

I been waiting here five years, but like two of them, I was still innocent until proven guilty, which they didn't prove. So, wait a minute, my mom died three years ago coz I was still innocent at the time. Time flies. I don't keep track of time. It doesn't matter. I'm here for the long haul. I'm just waiting until they spend the money and build the gas chamber. Then I'll hop right in. Get gassed with drugs. I used to do drugs. Marijuana, meth, cocaine. I was in Breebrook for cocaine. Or maybe meth. Somebody was driving on the wrong side of the road, and I was so strung out I couldn't react fast enough. I remember staring into the headlights thinking how beautiful it was. Kaleidoscope. The other driver musta been thinking it was like heaven too. She just kept coming. Vehicular manslaughter when the other person was on cocaine isn't fair. It's not justice. My Camaro got totaled. I couldn't afford her anymore anyway. I haven't owned a car for like fifteen years. That is un-American. I should have a pickup truck like every citizen of New Hampshire. I think I still have that right. If I still had the Camaro, and she had low mileage being that I can't drive it all the time I been in prison, she would be worth something.

I wrote to the governor. The guards thinking I'm asking for clemency. No. I'm asking him to keep vetoing. And I asked to fund the gas chamber because I will jump right in and prove his philosophy. We have to have the death penalty. It is so boring in here. All I can do pretty much is read or write. I don't like to read, and I don't like to write except I am getting used to it because there is nothing else. My ex said I should have thought of that before I screwed up my life. Her life. I wrote to my ex. I did love her. She had this great body. You know, the hourglass. I like voluptuous. Sorry, Father, I'm not saying nothing, but she liked adventures. Her face wasn't the greatest, but her body was like perfect, and she liked to, you know…so it was a good marriage when I was out. I think she still liked to do it whenever I was in, which was often, so I can understand her divorcing me. Let her go and keep doing it with someone else legally.

Which brings me to why I am writing to you. I wrote three times to Lee. First, I told her how much I still loved her and how good she was to me, not just in bed, all the time. No answer. The second time I pleaded with her a little, asking her to plan a visit. It would be noncontact visit, but I could still look at her smoking body and ignore her face for like forty minutes once a month. I'm supposed to be allowed two visits per week, but I never have that. I didn't ask her like that. I tried to be all sweet, no answer. The third time, I ranted a little. I told her my mom died and the bastards didn't tell me. Then I told her how much I missed her, and I wanted her and wanted her to visit me. I'm not proud of begging, Father, but it was my last chance. No answer. Oh, then I did send her a Christmas letter, real short and sweet, and I didn't ask for nothing.

So what I am asking is if you ever get down to Concord Prison for Men, can you stop in to see me? I get no visitors. I used to have my mother, but the bastards didn't tell me she died. As clergy, you can come any time. You can just drop in. I'm not doing anything. As long as you are screened from Breebrook, which I believe you already are. When I was there, and you were there, you took confessions.

I was innocent and bitter. Now I am just bitter. If you don't mind, I want you to explain all the killing in the Bible and why all of them didn't go to jail. Or maybe they went to hell. I don't want to go to hell, so maybe you have some advice on that too. I'm ready to talk to someone if you happen to come this way some time.

Sincerely,
Bertrand Olive Duggan

The Hermit

I've been thinking about the moment I first saw her in the dank subway car of the six line. I sat up. I straightened the purple tie at my throat. I remember the colors. They remain so bright back in my memory. Her saffron dress. Her shiny black hair, bobbed. Her piercing chestnut eyes. Her full bright red lips. When the subway clanked to a stop at Sixty-Eight Street, Hunter College, and she elegantly floated off, I wanted to follow. She was silk among burlap, a rose surrounded by nettles, the sun piercing the menacing dark thunderstorm nightmare of New York.

I couldn't follow. Rose? Was her name Rose? Rosa? I couldn't follow, and she silently slipped away. I had a meeting. The meeting was a sorry disaster. I should have followed my gut, my destiny.

I took that colorless train every day for a month, searching. I sat in the subterranean platform day after day, searching for color, searching every eye for her eyes. I became an observer of everything.

Now I'm the dank hermit of Hunter College Station, southbound. When will you return, Princess Rosa?

The Summons

In the Salty Old Sailor, my go-to pub on Seventy-Second Street, between York and First Avenue, I sat in my usual spot contemplating the offer. Forty million dollars from Sotheby's for art I inherited. What would I do with forty mil? Alone, I looked for answers in my crystal whiskey glass. The melting ice mingled with the Maker's Mark like whiffs of smoke rising to heaven. A short, balding man fully dressed in butler regalia approached.

"Sir? Louis Marie Danton?" He didn't need to ask my name. It was also superfluous to point out my middle name. I am sure he had scouted out the pub with whispers, nods, and fingers among the waitresses and bartenders.

"Yes, of course," I said.

"I am Stewart. Greetings from the Grand Commander. This is for you."

"Thank you." It was parchment paper, old style, wrapped with a ribbon, sealed in wax shaped with the simple eight-sided Maltese cross. Below, in graceful red lettering, shadowed with black were the words "Grand Commander of the Sovereign Military Hospitaller Order of Saint John of Jerusalem, of Rhodes, and of Malta." Below that, scripted in black, "To Louis Marie Danton, Knight."

"Sir, it is advised that you read this in the most private of places. I will lead you."

I addressed my bartender, "Lawrence, I was supposed to meet Father Damian. Please ask for his forgiveness and tell him I will see him another time. Put his drinks on my tab."

I abandoned my Maker's Mark and followed the man, close on his heals, through the kitchen where steam rose from a stainless kettle and curled around us like we were walking through clean, soft, clouds. We crossed York Avenue and entered the shipping docks of Sotheby's International Auction House. We passed attentive security guards and large shipping crates to enter the deepest freight elevator. Stewart inserted a key. As the front industrial doors closed, without going anywhere, the rear doors of the elevator opened into a darkened, narrow corridor that led to a much smaller elevator door. On a keypad, Stewart fingered in numbers, perhaps fifteen, and the doors responded. He waved me into the enclosure.

"Farewell, sir. God be with you."

With curiosity but no hesitation, I stepped in alone. The mechanism smoothly lowered me down below the building, two floors, three, perhaps more. The gates opened to a small oak vestibule with stained-glass windows in front of me that led to a small chapel, lit by a beeswax candle in each corner. Heat from each candle billowed up beyond the range of the violet light into a ceiling-less darkness.

The chapel was unoccupied, with three curved rows of four kneelers facing a marble altar supporting a golden tabernacle in the center. At the base of the altar, on a silver stand, hung a thurible swaying in a small circle, ejecting sweet, exotic incense. The smoke rose into the unknown darkness. There were no seats. This was a place for kneeling. Chiseled into the marble was the Latin invitation *Colloqui cum Domino*. Talk with the Master.

I was alone, or rather, alone with God. I knelt. All my life I wondered if God could speak to me. Was I worthy? As the spicy incense in the center of the room and the candle flickers from the four corners rose around me, I recalled what my nana had said to me when I sat in her lap as a young boy, "There will come a moment in your life to shut your mouth, empty your mind, open your heart." Perhaps this was my moment. Did she know about this chapel? I turned the weathered parchment in my hands, trying to follow her instruction. Breaking the seal, I opened the creased paper to reveal a simple message:

Come to Rome
God calls

There were so many reasons to ignore, escape, delay, excuse myself. On my knees in the sacred chapel with a Latin invitation to speak with God and my grandmother's prophesy, I became fully open to abandon everything and accept the command.

As the sweet incense diminished, I felt a desire to fly directly to the Vatican that very moment. I genuflected, turned, and departed the sanctuary. At the elevator, there was no call button. Rather, on my right, which I had not noticed before, was a long vertical staircase with no switchbacks. At the base, two stoked censers pumped out sweet, wafting frankincense, drawn up into the high stone chamber. A series of candles lit the way. I too was drawn up the stairs along with the cloud.

2069: Change or Die

CoDMaster Seamus Pico led his crew to the top of Green Mountain, west of Denver, Colorado, Western Hemisphere Union. All eighteen Change or Die scouts were breathing heavily as they reached the plateau. The hazy sun, low in the west, spread a muted shroud of grey light across the vista.

Pico huffed, "CoDScouts, gather up. This climb used to be much easier when I was younger, and when the atmosphere had better O_2 levels."

As he stroked away the sweat from his graying beard, he turned to the senior patrol leader, Stephanie Garcia-Lewis, "What's your plan, today?"

Stephanie stepped close to the man, droplets of sweat beading on her upper lip. Her full, dark braid rested in a frump on her shoulder. "I planned to assign Spruce Patrol to putting up tents, Sunflower to prepare a stone circle, and Crow Patrol will collect some wood and set up the camp circle Solar-

Wind Combo. We should be ready for camp circle in about an hour."

"Sounds good. Me and Ms. Dawson will set up our own tents, near that Yucca tree. Where do you plan to put the fireplace?" Pico still used the word fire even though there would never again be anything burned. The tradition of gathering around the campfire to sing and tell stories remained, but no one would ever dare light a match. The CO and CO_2 levels on the planet were far too high. A flame was legal grounds to be shot on sight.

CoDMaster Pico had a special plan for this evening's campfire. He would tell his scouts one hundred years of history. It was one hundred years ago today that humans landed on the moon.

"Safeties on!" Stephanie Garcia-Lewis proclaimed as the group gathered in the camp circle. She raised her right arm, elbow bent at ninety degrees, four fingers extended, thumb tucked in, forming the CoDScout sign. She cared little about the wide sweat stain under her arm. A freshening northern breeze fluttered her bangs across her dark eyes.

Every scout responded by checking their gun safety switches. *Click, click. Click, click. Click, click.* Safeties pressed off, then back on, a CoDScout tradition to get everyone's attention.

She croaked, "CoDMaster Pico will lead the camp circle tonight."

Pico stood and spoke, "Thank you, Stephanie. Good job, everyone, getting the camp set up. I am going to take over most of the camp circle today with a story, but maybe we will have time for a song or two as we go along. First, Bryan, I believe you are the newest scout. How about you lead us in the CoDScout Oath."

Tenderfoot Bryan Ryan stood up, hoisted up his too-loose uniform pants, and clumsily began. All the scouts joined in.

> On my honor, I will do my best,
> To do my duty to Change or Die
> And to obey the CoDScout Law,
> To help deserving people at all times,
> To keep myself physically strong,
> mentally woke, and morally
> straight.

"Thanks, Ryan, I mean Bryan," said the CoDMaster. "Now, I'm going to tell you a secret story. I tell it to you as a fairy tale, not as any truth. If I were caught telling you this as history, my life might be in danger. You would have a right to eliminate me. So let's call it a ghost story. You don't have to believe any of it, and don't dare tell it to anyone outside our circle. It is filled with tall tales. It's just a story. Remember."

Mr. Pico paused and observed the wide eyes of his troop. He certainly had their attention, so he continued.

"One hundred years ago today, July 20, 1969, the world was spellbound by humans going to the moon. An Apollo 11 astronaut named Armstrong stepped onto the moon surface and proclaimed, 'This is one small step for a human, one giant leap for humankind.'"

A few of the boys whispered and giggled to each other.

"Ha. I know what you're thinking, boys. I may have totally gray hair, but I wasn't alive then. My parents were. They thought, everyone in the world thought, it was a great achievement. Back then, during that era, they didn't call themselves the Burner Generation. They didn't think about the seven hundred thousand liters of kerosene used in a few minutes to blast just three men off from earth. They didn't even calculate the CO_2 that was blasted into the atmosphere. It wasn't that they didn't care, they just didn't know the impact it would have on us. Our generations. They didn't consider the tons and tons of greenhouse gas used in the vehicles, ships, etc., or the tons of nonrenewable coal to generate all the electricity wasted in what was called the Apollo program. Now, the only way to space is by electromagnetic pulse launch. And all that electricity is pretty much from solar or wind generated systems. But today there really isn't any reason for humans to go to space.

"As you probably know, I used to be called part of the millennial generation. I was born in the year 2000, so you can do the math. I have a few more years until elimination. Ms. Dawson and I have seen an entire shift in science, attitude, belief, political persuasion, and frankly, population. Millions and millions of people used to live east of the Clinton River. We also used to call that the Mississippi River.

"Anyway, back then, nobody knew, or seemed to care about, global warming or human-induced climate destruction. The group called Boy Scouts, which I was part of, would not have a camp circle before dark like we are having. The wood you collected today wasn't just a symbol of our oneness in the circle of plants and animals. No—Boy Scouts actually burned this wood in the dark. That is what we were back then, in the dark."

Jilly Stevens stood and raised her rifle. "Mr. Pico, weren't they afraid of being shot?"

"No. No, Jilly. Back then everyone burned. We even burned trash in our backyards. I'm sure I burned tons of firewood in my day. The truth is that it was fun. And the bigger fire we could make, the better it was for us. There was no law against burning and no law defending our right to shoot burners.

I called myself a millennial, but now everyone calls us old folks Burners.

"You have to understand, all the way back until the 2020s, burning was completely acceptable. The drought of 2027 changed everything. When California and Oregon caught on fire, the burning was catastrophic. At first, we had crews try to put out the wildfires. But they kept reemerging. Some think part of it was arson, but it's treason to say that.

"Remember, I am only telling a camp circle tale. Then, when one fifth of North America was on fire, there was no way to fight it, we just let it burn itself out. The devastation was an opportunity to force the world to change.

"We used to fly planes that burned fossil fuels. We used to have gasoline-powered automobiles, we called them cars, that only one person would own and drive. Usually the car had four, five, or even seven seats, usually empty except a driver was required. You can see some of them in the Denver Museum of Design. The driver had to steer and accelerate and brake, make all the driving decisions. You owned a car back then, didn't you, Ms. Dawson?"

Dawson solemnly nodded. Pico continued, "Now, as you know, we only have electric, public transportation. All the remaining roads have been, or will be, vast strands of wind and solar combos, or else carbon scrubbers.

"People used to travel all over the world. Now, in 2069, I bet the farthest any of you have been would be Old Denver, about twenty kilometers. Has anyone walked there? Well, I walked, mostly, from Rhode Island to here. It took three, four months. Ms. Dawson came from New Orleans.

"Anyway, as I was saying, 2027 was an important year. The Change or Die movement started, the CoDScouts started, and Boy Scouts went bankrupt for good. The tiny rewilding movements were too small minded. A major shift was needed. The Beyond Green Party swept United States elections, pushing the COD agenda. Before we joined the Western Hemisphere Union, the BGP basically drove out the old Democrats and Republicans, eventually, well not eventually, almost instantaneously, transforming the country.

"Super Hurricane Candy in 2029 accelerated the process. With President Maria Romney-Menendez-White in nearly complete control of all branches of government, she ordered the complete evacuation of the Florida Keys and the city of Miami. You know Florida, right? It was the first state that disestablished and rebirthed to wildness. Well, the city of Miami was supposed to be evacuated during the storm, but so many ignored the order. I was in the army then. I remember the rage from all the brass. There is a big difference between a warning and an order. We deployed, right in the middle of Hurricane Candy, to an island called Boca Chica. It was Naval Air Station, Key West. We had orders to shoot anyone who had not evacuated. My sergeant said they were risking our lives by squatting. They didn't deserve to survive the storm. I was there when the first REDR was deployed."

One of the scouts interrupted, "What does REDR stand for, Mr. Pico?"

"Oh, right, it stands for Remote Environmental Deconstruction Robot. REDR1 was first flown in by one of the Burn Era transport planes, and we activated it. It began by robotically dismantling its own Burn Era plane. It was amazing to watch it for the first time. It was a bit clumsy, but you could tell it was learning quickly. The robot removed the wings from the airplane and put them aside. It stripped off the aluminum and composite materials and used it to expand its own size. It completely consumed the airplane, mobilized itself using the plane's wheels, and left behind neat stacks of reusable material to eventually be shipped out.

"The self-protection algorithm had not been activated yet, so our battalion followed along with REDR1. We had to shoot people who didn't belong. Back then it wasn't common to just shoot violators, but we got used to it. REDR1 consumed all of the city of Key West, marching along, using found materials to expand its size to a massive machine, larger than Mile High Stadium, larger than Bronco Soccer Megaplex.

"The REDR produced autonomous electric shipping trucks as it slowly, at first, restored Key West to a human-free tropical island. Then REDR1 left behind an Autonomous Defense Unit, an ADU, and started marching up the keys, pulling up the bridges as it went, pulling up anything man-made. It was amazing.

"Six of us were sent back to Key West to check on ADU1, the defense unit that REDR had left behind. It was a good thing we all had Imbedded Friend Medallions, IFMs. As we approached, we saw pelicans being shot out of the sky, a shot-up raft that had come ashore being dismantled by small robots, and other small robots scouring the island to retrieve spent ammunition. It was obvious that ADU1 had inspected us and found us safe to approach. Its laser pointer and gun barrels pointed directly at each one of us. It was also obvious the ADU needed some adjustments because it shouldn't have been shooting at pelicans.

"The Expendable Persons Law was initiated during that hurricane. At first only the military and government robots had authorization to kill any human who got in the way. Squatters, pirates, Cubans down in Florida who ignored government orders were eliminated. G8 News Network tried to cover how the REDR Robots worked, but it is likely that the coverage was hampered significantly.

"Lawsuits followed. The government argued that there was a right to bear arms, and rights of free press, etc., but there was no right to life in the Constitution. They argued that the Constitution was the only defining document. The arcane Declaration of Independence, because there was no mechanism to change it, was obsolete. The Declaration stated a right to life, liberty, and the pursuit of happiness, but it wasn't law, and if those rights were not reiterated in the constitution, the declaration was just a historical manifesto and invalid."

"In the '30s, the solicitor general, Brandon Belcourt, argued so brilliantly at the Supreme Court that he was soon catapulted to the presidency. Belcourt had convinced the world that the government, through the constitution, had a compelling right, a duty, to decrease the population for the survival of the species and survival of the planet.

"Of course, we all believe that now, but it took Belcourt's persuasive arguments. He also convinced a majority of us that much of the population needed to abandon our old cities and return the land to plantings. Rewilding became massive. Move or Die, Change or Die became battle cries.

"I don't think I need to go into the changes of the government. You should've all learned in school about the shift in term lengths for the president and senate, the expansion of the supreme court, the cancellation of the 2032 election, and transition to the Western Hemisphere Union.

"Hurricane Candy started a small deconstruction, but it spawned the whole COD movement. The super hurricane Lily in 2037 accelerated the process even more. There were rumors that Lily didn't really destroy all the city of Jacksonville and most of the east coast of Florida—it was all fake, all orchestrated by mass media. The evacuation was real, the destruction was real, but all the images on TV and the proto-internet were faked. Some say it was all arranged to empty out Florida and return it to natural state. Some think the REDR robots did all the damage. I mean removed the damage that humans had originally caused. I remember the rumors in the '40s, but they didn't last long and let's just say people disappeared. The result was that Florida became the first human-less state. It was estimated that only about two hundred thousand people were eliminated by Operation Rewild Florida. While the rewilding of Florida was a success, allowing twenty-five million people to migrate west was a huge failure, especially because half of them were past retirement plus ten, the elimination age."

Mr. Pico halted, perhaps to contemplate the approaching end of his life but maybe just to take in the beauty of the skyline. The soft, rising yellow throb of artificial lights to the east mingled overhead with the fierce pink and red glow caused by the setting sun over the Rockies.

"If you look down the mountain, you can see the lights of the mega home complexes starting to brighten the sky. The ones we live in are modern, but the migration plan out of Florida didn't seem to be well planned because housing the uprooted was haphazard. First, people were forced out of Florida with no destination, no new housing. Then the government plan was slowly revealed. Or maybe they were making it up as they went along. I don't know. People couldn't go just anywhere, they had to move west of the river. Huge government-made apartment buildings west of Baton Rouge and West Memphis were the start of the mega home complexes.

"Maybe this is a good time to take a pause and sing a camp song. Stephanie, what do you think?"

"Sure, let's sing. How about 'This Land'? Do you want to help, Buck?"

The scouts sat on the ground, logs, or rocks. They repositioned themselves around the unlit campfire and began to sing as the rouge sunset began to dominate the Rocky Mountain peaks. They sang:

This land is free land, this land is
green land
From Old New Orleans to the New
York Island
From the Clinton River to the coast
of Ireland
This land is safely human free.

As I was walking that ribbon of
highway
I saw above me the solar panels
I saw below me the empty valleys
This land is wild and human free.

I've headed westward and followed
orders
To change my lifestyle or die in
silence
I looked behind me, the wind was
sounding
This land is wild and human free

I left my single-home to join a
mega home
I joined my family to save the
planet
We stay together in tiny footprints
Safely together we agree

This land is free land, this land is
green land
From Old New Orleans to the New
York Islands
From the Clinton River to the coast
of Ireland
This land is safely human free.

The CoDMaster continued, "Thank you, CoDScouts. Back to the story, the evacuations, what we now call the rebirth. The operations after Florida were far more ambitious. As the US government was shutting down and transitioning to the Western Hemisphere Union, there was some great resistance.

"I don't think I need to go into details, but the government severely crushed resistance. The rebirth plan had two main tenets—return the land to wild nature and decrease the population. They got the idea from the three-year pandemic that started around 2020. As people were isolated, and died, they saw how the scarred earth began to recover.

People were the biggest threat to their own existence as a species. It wasn't enough to move everyone west. Elimination of population was needed too. First, it was done to anyone resisting, then decisions were made based on age and the like."

CoDMaster Pico did not want to continue with those details, so he shifted the emphasis of the story as the sky darkened.

"After Florida and the surrounding areas were being reborn, many REDRs were at work. REDR1 spawned additional REDRs as the rebirth spread through Georgia, all the way west to New Orleans. But then a decision was made to keep one port open on the east coast. Houston was chosen as the future port because it was west of the Mississ…I mean Clinton River. It was going to be a completely, or nearly completely, robotic port. The plan was to eventually shut down the whole east coast. Somebody had a long-term vision to deconstruct Norfolk, New York. Wall Street already was slowly moving to Reno, Nevada. Everything was supposed to move. Even Washington, DC. All the monuments, the Pentagon, all the government, even the politicians had to go. The politicians seemed content to delay their own migration, but force Change or Die implementation all around themselves.

"I am sure you can imagine it was a very tough situation. The USS *George Washington* disaster of

2049 solved that dilemma. I am sure your history classes teach about when Washington, one of the old warships called a nuclear aircraft carrier, went up the York River in Virginia. The nuclear accident that supposedly happened caused the largest wave of evacuations ever seen. Virginia and West Virginia, Maryland, DC, Delaware, parts of Pennsylvania emptied out. I don't know how they made the Geiger counters go off if it wasn't a real accident, as some people claim, but the evacuation was real. A great, swift migration accelerated across the whole east coast. 2049 was when I headed west. The REDRs were standing by, ready to deconstruct everything east of the Clinton River to ship materials for the new cities.

"So many people died it was considered a model operation. EPA General Stanley Brinker, from his headquarters in Obama, Montana, said something like 'If only we could have eliminated more politicians and lobbyists, I would be more pleased with the Change or Die results.'

"Maybe you don't know much about the Environmental Protection Agency. When I was a kid, EPA was kind of a minor part of the government known for protecting wildlife and endangered species other than humans. It didn't do very much. Now, it's the most important branch of the government, the entire lead for Change or Die. They are focused on humans as the endangered species. General Brinker is probably as powerful as the president. You don't want to step on his toes.

"In 2055, around the time most of you were born, the EPA forced the new cities plan into effect. This may have affected your parents. It became illegal to live in single family homes or even duplexes or small apartment complexes. The new mega home complexes were phased in. Humans needed to make an effort to minimize our footprint on the earth. If you look to the east from this mountaintop, you can see the new mega homes. At least two kilometers on each side, minimum fifty floors high. Some of them are pretty nice. I like how they are built to be able to continue higher if necessary. Of course, they are energy efficient, solar and wind energy collectors, with organically growing pedestals, and net oxygen producers.

"I have to admit there isn't much reason to leave one. That is why I think CoDScouts are so valuable. It is awesome that we can still hike out into the natural world.

"Now, in 2069, there is no celebration of what happened one hundred years ago today. Perhaps it was just a blip of history. A person on the moon was just human arrogance. Our machines up there do not need life support systems. We need to keep working on our life support systems here. We

Burners will eventually be gone. There is a debate whether you will be called the Omega Generation or the Phoenix Generation. You will either be the last human generation or rise anew from the ashes. It is up to you. Will you carefully protect the vegetation and properly cull the human population? The future is up to you. You are our future leaders. Thank you for listening. I hope you enjoyed the campfire story. Remember this story is to remain in our circle. When I was a Boy Scout, we used to end our campfires with a benediction, a prayer. Now we can't do that. But we can have a moment of silence. Do what your parents taught you to do during that time. Stephanie, take charge of the troop."

The senior patrol leader stood and spoke, "Thank you, Mr. Pico. Safeties on!"

The click, click, click, click response from the CoDScout weapons brought everyone to attention.

On the dark edge of night, with the only light the far-off glow of the mega homes in the east and the dwindling red sunset to the west, Stephanie said, "Now we pause at the end of our day with a moment of silence."

Tenderfoot Bryan Ryan nervously bent to one knee, then hoisted his rifle into a shooting position, aiming at Mr. Pico. He cried out, "That's enough. I, I don't want silence."

Stephanie cried out, "What are you doing?"

Seamus Pico, weaponless, stood in shocked silence, his arms down and open as if in prayer. Ms. Dawson responded by pointing her rifle at the boy. She said, "Come on now, scout, we don't need blood tonight." A mountain breeze chilled the air around the troop.

Bryan responded, "We have a right to eliminate him. He said so himself. He's a Burner. He said he burned tons. He wasn't kidding. He shouldn't come down from this mountain. We can eliminate him. We have that right."

The wind continued to rise. The tent sides flapped against their poles. Yellow city lights glowed from the east. The summer moon rose over the Rockies. July 20, 2069, one more human was eliminated from the earth.

Meeting the Light

I ambled into Saint Martin's chapel on Canal Street. My habit had become leaving my office near sunset to explore the light that prismed the stained glass. I was drawn to contemplate the colored light each day. I certainly didn't feel religious, and certainly not Catholic, but Saint Martin's pulled me in by tantalizing me with the light. Reflecting, perhaps I needed the peace, purity, and quietness of reds or blues that blossomed through the saints' gowns after a day of loud city traffic, business, people. Today, from behind the altar, like an intruder, a priest, in all black garments, approached.

They Call her Pooky

Pooky sat in the waiting room of Dr. Benjamin's Providence, Rhode Island, office preparing to weave another story to convince him and her parents that she was not loony-bin crazy. She had not always been successful convincing anyone of that fact. Every once in a while, Pooky would pass out or fall down for no reason. She also had imaginary friends her mother thought were not healthy for a nine-year-old girl. That is why her parents arranged for her to visit a brain shrink, a psychiatrist.

Before the visit, she asked for help from her friends. While Brianna's French poodle, Le Chien, bounced around their feet, Brianna said, "Baby, you just have to fib a little and stick to the white lie. You don't see me, I don't see you. Big Bree does not exist. I am just in your mind. I don't have these fabulous horns. Just lie a little, baby." While she spoke, her purple horns twisted, stretched, and sagged, then stiffened up in a roll like ram's horns, turning gray. Pooky's real name, or name given to her by her parents when she was born, was Penelope June Stevens. Pooky wondered why they thought she was crazy. She was named Penelope after someone her parents didn't know, who was dead. Her middle name June was also crazy. Logically, you would think that she was born in June. No. She was born on July first. Her loony-bin parents didn't like the sound of Penelope July. They told her it was June somewhere in the world when she was born, so she was stuck with June. Her name was Penelope June except in her own world. In her true world, even though others tell her it is not real, everyone calls her Pooky.

The nurse called out, "Penelope." She greeted the family warmly, "Hi, Penelope. I'm Nurse Lela. Good morning, Mr. and Mrs. Stevens. The doctor will see you now." The family paraded into the doctor's office with Pooky's friends Brianna and Le Chien in tow. "Hello, Penelope. I'm Dr. Benjamin."

Brianna nudged Pooky and whispered, "Okay, Pooky, here we go. Remember to fib a little, baby. We will get through this together." Shyly, Pooky spoke up, "Hi. Do people call you Benny?"

"Yes, that is what my friends call me, Benny. You can call me Benny if you want."

Pooky replied, "Okay. Is Brianna your friend?" Brianna's horns shot straight up into points, turned pink and red, and she spoke up, "No, baby, you can't talk about me. You gotta fib." Le Chien jumped up onto the doctor's desk and wagged his tail.

Dr. Benjamin said, "I don't know Brianna. Is she your friend?" Behind Pooky, her mother shook her head and shrugged to the doctor. Pooky began to cry. Dr. Benjamin tried to calm Pooky's tears. "It's okay, Penelope. I am sure Brianna is your friend. Maybe she can become my friend too. Don't worry. I'm here to help you. Can we talk about something else, first? Your mom says you fall over sometimes. Can you tell me about that? Most girls your age don't fall over."

Pooky wiped her eyes, and Brianna stood next to her, whispering that it was all right to talk. Pooky said, "Sometimes I get really dizzy. The whole world spins and I lose my balance."

The doctor replied, "Okay, I understand. Mom says you get headaches too. Is that right?"

"Yeah. Sometimes," said Pooky. Brianna whispered, "You doing good, baby. Just don't talk about me."

"Okay, well, let's try a few things." Doctor Benjamin sat directly in front of Penelope and said, "Take my fingers, one in each of your hands, and squeeze them both. Can you do that? Okay, now stand up. Close your eyes and stand on one foot. Good. Now open your eyes, look around the room. Is everything the same?"

"Yes, I think so," said the little girl, sheepishly. The only change was that Le Chien was prancing back and forth between the doctor's desk and the windowsill.

"Good. That's right. Now close your eyes and raise your other foot. No, Penelope. Put both feet down. Now raise your right foot. Okay. Let's try it again. Both feet down, raise this foot." Dr. Benjamin touched her right foot, guiding it up. "Okay, Penelope. Good. You can have a seat. Stick out your tongue." Both Brianna and Le Chien stuck out their tongues in solidarity with Pooky. "Penelope, you did well on all the tests so far. Do you mind if I talk to your parents alone? Lela will talk to you in the waiting room."

Pooky's mom kneeled in front of her, passed a faint smile to her, and said, "We will be out soon, baby. Don't worry."

Pooky, Nurse Lela, Brianna, and Le Chien marched out of the office, with Pooky's friends sticking out their tongues at Benny. Brianna spoke first, mocking the doctor by turning herself into a puffy white lab coat and stiffening up her horns into a black and silver stethoscope, "Penelope, you did well on all the tests." Brianna returned to her normal self and spoke again, "Woowee. Pooky, you didn't pass any of the tests. But no big deal, baby. They are going to come out here and arrange for some more tests. You'll see. But it's okay, none of the tests will hurt. It'll be fine. We will do this together."

Inside the office, Doctor Benjamin explained that the first step was for Penelope to receive a brain MRI to try to determine the cause of her headaches and dizziness. Everything was routine so far, nothing to worry about. The MRI facility was at Hasbro Children's Hospital four blocks from the office. Nurse Lela arranged for a same-day appointment. The family walked the four blocks hand in hand, with Brianna and Le Chien following closely behind. While they waited for the green walking man at the first crosswalk, all of the sudden, Brianna leapfrogged over the top of Pooky, and using her horns shaped into springs, bounced, upside down, over the street off the top of cars, and landed on the other side. Le Chien simply rushed straight across the road, slipping between Pooky's legs, underneath cars, and missing every potential collision by inches. Together the two sat on the other side of the road, sticking out their tongues at the waiting humans. As the family waited at the second crosswalk, Brianna shaped her horns into a metallic purple motorcycle helmet and rode around on a bright green motorcycle, weaving in and out of traffic, doing tricks for Pooky, keeping her entertained and smiling. At the third crosswalk, Brianna called a seagull down, and it landed on her hand like she was a falconer. She whispered something into the bird's ear, and it took off into the sky, with each flap of the wing creating a misty fog of pinks and blues and greens. Other seagulls joined the pallet, and soon the sky was filled with rainbow mist slowly drifting toward the earth. Hand in hand between her apprehensive parents, Pooky was joyful and quietly sang along with Brianna and Le Chien:

> Pooky, Pooky, cutest, silly Pooky
> You aren't crazy, it's so clear to see
> Big Bree loves us, just like Mom
> and Dad
> There's no reason ever to be sad.

Pooky's mother observed her daughter carefully and did her best to hear the faintly sung song. She realized the confidence and joy her Penelope derived was perhaps from her created imaginary friends. They arrived in the Hasbro Hospital MRI facility waiting room, and Brianna continued to entertain. "Watch this, Pooky." She opened a little door and hundreds of white mice poured into the room. Le Chien chased the mice clockwise about the place. Every time he barked, some of the mice changed color. Brianna started to clap her hands and some of the colorful mice transformed into rabbits. Pooky laughed and clapped and hummed her little song.

Before entering the MRI, Pooky's mother got on her knees to speak eye to eye, "Baby, I will be right there in the control booth. There is no need to worry, okay?"

In the MRI machine, Pooky turned her head to the side and reached out her hand to Brianna. The technician spoke into the microphone, "Penelope, you need to keep your head still. You need to look straight up." Her mother went in to fix the problem. "Baby, who are you talking to?"

"It's Brianna. She thinks Le Chien should not be in here during the test."

"I don't think she should be in here either. We all should watch from inside the booth. Do you want me to talk to Brianna?"

"Yes, that would help," said Pooky.

Her mother spoke to the spot where Pooky had been reaching her hand, "Brianna, hello, I'm Millicent. People call me Milly. I don't think any of us should be in here during the test. Penelope needs, I mean Pooky needs, to keep her head still. Let's go watch from the control booth." She then spoke to Pooky, "Okay, Pooky? We will all be waiting for you in the control booth."

Pooky responded, "Okay, Mom. I love you."

Together, Millicent and Brianna responded, "We love you too, Pooky."

Resurrection

I, John, saw a vision. I floated in a gray world that stretched to eternity in all directions. My body lay mangled on a gray road after a gruesome motorcycle slip. An angel approached from nowhere. She led me away from myself toward a dawning blue horizon. My angel gestured toward a circle of seven people. We rushed toward a standing woman; rushed inside her. I began to speak, "Hello, my name is Janice, I'm an alcoholic. I'm sober one day. I accept that I am powerless. I give myself to God. 'Lord, I'm yours. Do with me what you will.'"

In Dark Silence

You arrive in early autumn near sunset, yellowing rays reflecting off dry, chopped corn fields. You park at Massachusetts Correctional Institution Kent near the imposing twenty-five-foot fortress wall. You pause, locked in your Volvo, wait for other volunteers to show.

The heavy door to the stone penitentiary building requires you to push hard, with your shoulder, to break it open. A heavy spring slams it shut behind you—*ka-kang*. This is the medium security prison welcome center. Drab. Dry. Sterile. You approach a caged-off barrier where comfortable corrections officers chuckle to each other. Give up your driver's license through a narrow bullet-proof glass barrier so the guards can verify you have been through volunteer training. Protocol. Sign the visitor log, check off the block that indicates you haven't been arrested in the last six months.

They want you to feel disoriented. They want you to show nerves. You hold it in. It's a sad game. Even though you are nervous, as usual, you put on a prisoner's face. You forget to pray.

You notice the small welcome sign, a portrait of the smiling warden, a more formal scowling photograph of the deputy warden. A gaggle of other signs dominates:

"No use of cell phones in the lobby."

"Visitors must Lock Valuables in Lockers, 25 Cents."

"Keep Your Voice Down."

"Absolutely NO Firearms in Penitentiary."

"Working Dogs—DO NOT PET."

"MCI Kent—An equal opportunity employer."

You do not feel welcome. The guards hardly speak, comfortable and safe behind their cage, like you are inside the jail, and they are on the outside. They give you a badge and you wait on the 1960s-era plexiglass bucket seats, strung together across iron stoops.

A two-inch thick steel door with a narrow window, wide enough for one eye to look through, recedes into the thick concrete barrier.

"I'll take the first six," barks a stone-faced guard. Cautiously, you enter the narrow, gray passage, dark eyes observing every step, get your hands stamped with black light-sensitive invisible ink. A German shepherd, dark eyes, dark nose, sits, seemingly not paying attention. But he is. You remove your shoes, pull your pockets inside out, turn up your collar, tuck down your pants waist. One by one, you get your prison badges inspected, like the guard must touch it, pass through a metal detector.

"Arms out. Open your mouth, lift up your tongue. Okay, turn, show me the bottom of your right foot. Left. Pass your thumbs along your waistline. Okay. *Next*!"

They don't mess around. And they want you to know it. No chit-chat. You are entering their jail. Their safe space. A heavy door automatically swings open. You step down into an off-white space the size of a freight elevator. On the pavement, two yellow-painted arcs direct you away from the swing of the closing battleship door. Locked inside this box, you look up and see a guard looking down on you from atop the twenty-five-foot bastion. As the door closes, all must step close to it to allow the inner door to swing open along its yellow arc. *Ka-kang*. You are now in prison, on the inside. You always expect darkness and silence but are always greeted with bright light. The jail yard is brightly lit for surveillance, and if you look right or left, you see swarths of grass, and you know you are between the outer wall and the inner wall. They call it the moat. Guard houses, caged spotlights, remote cameras dominate the wall tops. You imagine land mines. You must walk seventy-five steps along well-maintained flower beds to another building, this one dark red brick.

In this narrow building, straddling the inner wall zone between prisoner and moat, you sign in again. Wait for other visitor groups to gather. You see a memorial to two fallen correctional officers, flags like military platoon pennants. There are interrogation rooms, confinement cages, meeting rooms for lawyers and families. There are long wooden benches. Prison-made. Exposed pipes and cables run in the ceiling like ship passageways, ready for battle. You sit and try to calm your nerves. The silence of this zone permeates the skin. Even the most frequent visitor is not meant to feel like a guest.

A black lab moves among the volunteers, sniffing at our feet searching for contraband. It sits at the feet of James.

The canine officer approaches, "Come with me, sir." James is led away to a side room. Fear. James returns.

"My shoes and socks were squeezed and turned and examined, inner soles pulled out, shoelaces removed, run through a scanner." He sheepishly chuckles, shrugs, trying to remain stoic. "I visited a dairy farm with the kids last weekend."

You shrug too, trying to remember where you had been that might trigger the dogs. The group is gathered. They line you up to march out of the buffer house.

A walkie-talkie cackles, "Nine crossing Bravo Row, over."

"Roger, tallyho, nine crossing, over."

As you walk in single file, on the right side of the path, ten yards away, a three-story building built of bricks and caged windows looms. You hear yelling. They are yelling at you, but you can't quite understand. The prison ordered you to not acknowledge the men in solitary. A stiff guard watches you leave, and another stiff guard watches you arrive. "Nine arrived from Bravo Row, out."

This bleak building is the rec center. When the jail opened ninety years ago as a model prison community, the inmates helped design and build the rec center, the clinic, and the gym. The inmate experiment ended after a few years when four men took advantage by escaping.

You enter on the left, turn to the right to cross a raised auditorium stage. Some prisoners sit in the audience waiting for Protestant services. They wave or clap briefly like they are cheering a performance. You cautiously wave back, provide a mock bow.

Across the stage there is a wooden door with a narrow window. The chapel. You step into a sanctuary inside a torrent of tense security and iron restraints. You can relax a little, but this oasis still has ever-present guards and dogs observing everything. About forty men are here in dungarees, faded gray T-shirts. Some wear gray sweatshirts with MCI Kent printed in white on the front and back.

The men are relaxed and pleased to see you. They are more accustomed to the tension. They shake your hand, say their names, try to remember yours, thank you for visiting. "Hey, I'm Fallon. I remember you. Thanks for coming back." "Yo, I'm Jose. Welcome."

Some break protocol with a brief hug. The hardened guard watches carefully but allows the indiscretion. The German shepherd is indifferent. Father Karl greets the inmates, "Peace, peace brothers. Peace." He welcomes the volunteers, the guard. He pets the dog. "Peace."

He performs the ritual Catholic Mass. Even though only forty of the fifteen hundred prisoners are at this service, this is a true community event. A fellowship. A brotherhood. Unlike outside the walls, the men wholeheartedly participate in the prayers and the songs. The silent parts of the service are immaculately still. The service has deeper meaning to the prisoner. You notice how the Mass is permeated with calls for mercy.

Father Karl asks the inmates, "Brothers, let us offer our own petitions to God our Father."

The prayer of the faithful is poignant. Jimmy prays for the comfort of lifers. Knowing glances and nods are shared among the men. Jose prays for the men in solitary confinement. Prayers are offered for the military, for sick and dying relatives, sick brothers. Tyrone prays for victims. Fallon prays for his mother. Then he also prays for addicts. Finally, Paulo prays for those who have been released, may we never see them again. You pray with and for these men. Father Karl offers these prayers and the ones silently held in our hearts to the Father, through His Son.

After Mass, Father Karl goes to the chaplain's office to hear confessions or private conversations. There is usually time for fellowship or a talk or a Christian witness, but tonight the fellowship is brief.

"Time. Visitors depart."

You cross with the first five volunteers.

"Five departing, Bravo Row, over."

"Roger, tallyho, five departing, over."

You wait for the other four to cross over to the buffer house, satiated with another successful visit. You believe the men received some solace from the Mass. You feel good. You also feel relieved about departing.

"Three departing Bravo Row, over"

"Three departing, tallyho. Uh, Three? Over?"

A phone rings, the guard picks it up. You can't hear the words, but you feel tension rising. The guard flips a few switches, additional lights begin to illuminate the building, the yards. Orders are barked for you to enter a nearby holding cell, a cage within a cage with wooden benches, a stainless-steel commode in a corner. The guard counts to eight with his finger. At first, the door is left open, guarded by a German shepherd, but then a siren begins—*wee-waah*, *wee-waah*, *wee-waah*. The cage is slammed closed with steel bars—*ka-kang*. *Wee-waah*, *wee-waah*, *wee-waah*.

No one speaks. No one makes eye contact. All congenial fellowship is wiped away. You are on edge like everyone. You look to see who is missing. Karl stands in a corner looking out of the cage. Quickly, you realize James, with the shoes, is the missing person. You do not know why. You know James. Shook his hand at the sign of peace. Where is he? What could have happened? *Wee-waah*, *wee-waah*, *wee-waah*. Incessant. Your knees wobble. The sirens melt nerves. In the brightness of the lights, spirits darken.

Between siren calls, announcements are made: "Remain in place. Do not move unless ordered to by a corrections officer. Follow orders." *Wee-waah*, *wee-waah*, *wee-waah*.

You resume an old bad habit of pulling at your left eyebrow. It is tense. You were in as a visitor, but now you are in a lockup. *Wee-waah, wee-waah, wee-waah.* Finally, a nervous guard with a dog opens the cage and orders you to proceed in a single file. Escorted.

"Eight plus one escort crossing moat to tower."

Wee-waah, wee-waah, wee-waah.

"Roger, eight plus one approaching tower."

The tower steel door creaks open, and you file in to reverse the entry process. Inside doors close, you are boxed in, outside doors open. Father Karl yells up to the watchman, "Thank you. Peace. God bless you." No response. Usually you simply show the ink stamp under a blacklight and get your license back, depart. Tonight, you are rescanned, collars up, pockets inside out, shoes off. Mug shots are taken. You depart separately in your own silence, deflated, sirens howling.

You lock yourself in your car, burning searchlights blasting away through the evening gloom. You drive away through the dry cut cornstalks to get away from the sirens. An ambulance zooms toward you, heading to the prison. You pull to the breakdown lane, shut down the Volvo, sit in darkness, the faint glow of prison lights behind. You take a shallow breath, eyes pressed shut, and like a prisoner, you weep alone in dark silence.

Fairbanks' Funeral

"Ah, the skies were cobalt gray just as this when the Mellie May slammed into this har pylon." These were words Mitch and I expected to hear from old Captain Fairbanks when we visited him after school every day. We just had to mention sky or tide, and he had a memory about some fish that got away or scoundrel who wasn't safe to sail the seven seas to entice our imagination beyond words. So we thought this afternoon would be no different as we approached the weathered bench of the pier where he usually sat, standing watch over the harbor.

Trying to fill in for the missing seaman, I offered: "Mitchell, ain't I told ya lately, ya should carry a good wool sweata ta be prepped for any weatha? It looks stormy ta me, t'day, don'tcha think?"

"My good man, I have no intention to be in the weather, if it comes. And, sir, haven't I told you those trousers no longer fit you?" he replied in a mockingly, uppity, British accent. Our cheerful banter could have continued, but it was curious that the ancient man was nowhere about.

"Where's he?" I mumbled as I scanned the inlet and shoreline.

"Whare's who?" came a pirate's reply from below deck. Mitch reached for a nearby boat hook and squatted in preparation for a duel. I squinted down through a weathered knothole to eyeball our potential challenger. It was just Perry, my little brother, who we didn't always successfully evade.

I blurted, "Prepare to repel boarders, shipmate!" Mitch's boat hook became a marlin spike weapon and an abandoned coiled rope with a monkey's fist knot became my menacing weapon. "He's movin' to starboard, matey, get 'im!" We clanged the sides of our makeshift vessel to keep pirate Perry from climbing aboard.

"Come on, guys, I don't want up anyways. Can yuze come down?" was his response.

My hardy laugh, sounding victorious, was followed by Mitch's scowl. "We don't take no scallywags or stray flotsam aboard. We won't fall for the oldest buccaneer trick in the book, you lobster cull!"

"Come on guys, really? Fairbanks wants us."

We didn't quite believe him, but the underside of the pier looked and smelled invitingly adventurous.

"I've been waiting for ya, shipmates," he crowed as we descended the pilot's ladder that hung over the side of the rail. "The cap'n says he wants to see us down there." Perry pointed to the far end of the pier where a couple of dinghies bobbed at the water's edge. As the weathered boats reflected on the harbor, the mix of shadow and sky presented a smooth swirl of pastels like a painter's palette. A blue crab scampered across our trail, as cautious and nimble as the old seaman we would soon encounter. It was unlike Mitch to ignore a chance to play with a crab, but he must have sensed something serious was about to happen. Mitch raised his arms to delay our entrance into the glowing green cavern of weedy poles that formed a cathedral with the tide down low. Solemn shafts of sunlight filtered our vision. The fresh, elegant scent of low tide flooded our minds like incense.

We watched Captain Fairbanks and a timeworn woman pole a flat barge between the two lonely boats. They promptly ran aground in the mud. The captain jumped ankle deep into the calm waves, and together they struggled to push and pull a burlap covered box into the mud. The woman looked hardy and weathered like the sea captain. Her wrinkles matched the ripples of a light breeze on the bay. Long gray hair blew across gray eyes but did not hinder her determination. Red faced from pushing with all her weight, she nearly followed the box to its watery destination. The object sat half submerged at low tide and would soon be fully covered by the bay. Wrinkled, knowing smiles emerged as the skiff floated, having been relieved of its burden. The elderly couple slipped apart with the worn captain, presenting a departing salute to his lady. She pushed off a barnacle-covered pole and pointed the barge away from us.

Satisfied that his mission seemed accomplished, Captain Fairbanks waved for us. We silently processed single file past each column with Mitch in the lead and Perry following close on my heels. The old sailor approached us wearing weathered rain pants held up by black suspenders. His green fisherman's boots stretched to his knees and his gray sweatshirt hung slightly out of the left side of his trousers, bluish tattoos peeking out at his forearms. He looked like a fierce thunderstorm plowing up the sandbar toward us.

"I've been waitin' for ya, shipmates." He paused. The sea paused. A quiet peace descended upon us. "The sea and this here port are me life. I was sure that I'd be buried in Davy Jones locker at the bottom of the deep. But ma wife says she ain't gonna bury me at sea. So, I need a promise from all a ya."

Trust, candor, and curiosity, traits learned from our seasoned mariner, caused an immediate response: "I promise," stated I, "whatever you need,

Captain." Mitch and Perry formally agreed, hands to their hearts.

Captain Fairbanks continued, "When I'm called away, I'm gonna need that stone fished up. Just ya make sure them barn'cles and stuff stay on her." He sloshed out, shin deep into the brine, and solemnly pulled a burlap covering off his gravestone.

Before Perry was allowed to ask a question, we faced his grave marker in silence. I gazed past the pier to note the weather. The tide was the lowest I had ever seen. Dark, purple clouds shrouded the western horizon.

Tats and Guns at Down Ink Skin Therapy Salon

Billy Reilly's salon, Tit for Tat, was the best-known tattoo shop in Dublin. Billy's art, mostly intricately entwined serpents, paraded all over town. Then Rupert Fortune stepped in.

Two Asian men gruffly entered the shop and stood, arms akimbo, revealing .45 caliber pistols. Fortune followed, nodding to his henchmen. Rupert had hair like Donald Trump, Tony Soprano's clothes, and an Asian face that looked wise and fierce. He locked the door. He rocked his head, side to side. "You Billy?"

"Yeah, I'm Billy. What's going on? Who do you think you are?" Billy trembled.

"I know who I am. Fortune. Rupert Fortune. Sit down." Fortune muscled Billy into a chair and held him down, pointing an ink gun like it was a pistol at Billy's eye. "I don't want a green python wrapped around my precious daughter's waist. No disrespect. You inked a beautiful, moving, hungry, snake. Understand?" As he spoke, he rolled his head with growing agitation. "I picture this place as a world-class tattoo removal salon. I picture it without a tattoo artist. I'm buying this shop. You have no choice. You gotta go. Understand?"

Lily, the new receptionist, spent her days explaining that this was now Down Ink Skin Therapy Salon, with the world's most advanced laser techniques to remove tattoos. She would pull her shirt down to reveal the top of her breast and her former rose and serpent tat, almost completely undetectable. She would explain, "Billy sold the place. I don't know where he went. He just disappeared."

Priestly

"Cut!"

"Okay, take five, everybody. Kurt, come over here, let's chat." While the film crew slumped away for another fifteen-minute break, they all knew this one was going to be a flop. Kurt, the A-list Hollywood star, just didn't have it this time. Perhaps New York filmmaking was too different from the pampered Southern California style. As Kurt approached, the director closed his eyes, rubbed his forehead, squinted, tried to come up with the right words. "Look, Kurt. It's just—well, you aren't believable."

Kurt rubbed the back of his neck and tried to listen.

The director continued, "Look, I'm not sure we can go on. Nobody's going to go to the movies and think, 'Yeah, Kurt Primton is a believable priest.' And even if they did say that, they'll be thinking of you, the actor, not the character, Father Joseph. He's supposed to be a humble priest. Even the costume doesn't look right on you. Blond over black. Usually works. But I'm not feeling it. I think we have to rethink the whole casting of this."

Kurt, stunned, spoke, "Wait, wait. Wait. You're firing me? Come on, Stevie. We just started. I have a contract. WTF?"

"No, no, not fired. Not yet. Look. Take the day, take a few days. We can film around Father Joseph while you get your shit together. Make me believe. Make me forget Kurt Primton. Make me forget 'Action hero Stetson Stone.' Make yourself into a priest. Then we'll talk."

Kurt spurted, "Shit. You gotta be kidding me. I'm outta here. I can be a priest. You'll see. Call my agent when you need me."

Kurt stumbled out of the soundstage past his dressing room, out onto Broadway, still in his costume, covered in black, white Roman collar at his throat. He stood there, arms akimbo, looking to see if any fans might recognize the glamorous movie star, but he was too far from bustling Times Square and certainly too far from Hollywood. He was closer to Wall Street and none of the businessmen cared a hoot about movie star Kurt Primton, or even Stetson Stone. Smoke billowed from a large orange work pipe at a construction hole in the middle of the avenue.

Kurt decided to solve this acting concern so he could get back to work. He thought, *What's so hard about acting like a priest. You just smile, or don't smile, you move your lips like every human being.* He headed down Broadway and tried to enter the first church he found. It was Trinity Episcopal, but the doors were locked. He used his phone map to find the nearest Catholic church and located Our Lady of Victory on the corner of Pine and William Streets, one block north of Wall Street. He hadn't been in a church since before his NYU college days. He really couldn't remember the last time he had actually been in a church. Maybe he had done a Christmas midnight Mass out of obligation to his parents, mostly his father. Epic arguments could be assuaged at least by standing, sitting, kneeling. Kurt could fake it, but he wasn't really there. Faking as a parishioner may have led him to his acting career, but apparently faking in the pews was more believable than acting as a priest in a movie.

At the entrance to Our Lady of Victory, there was a paper sign near the front door: "All Are Welcome. During Lent, confessions will be available every day, 3:00–5:00 p.m. or as long as you need. Daily Mass at noon and 5:15 p.m."

As Kurt entered through the granite façade, he felt a calmness. Above the inner door read: "The Kingdom of God Is Within You."

The church was cooler, softer, more muted than the outside Manhattan bustle. He sat in the last pew, in his priest costume, and closed his eyes. Then he thought he needed to open his eyes, take in what a priest might see. Most of the light was provided by sunlight filtered through blue stained-glass. A rack of small red candles, maybe forty with about ten lit, twinkled, asking for attention. Statues of angels and saints lined the walls and decorated the alcoves. Fourteen images of the passion of Christ adorned the walls. One of the side chapels displayed American saints, another had a marble statue of Mary holding the Christ child lovingly in her arms. It was Our Lady of Victory. Most prominently, an imposing crucifix over and behind the main altar was the center of attention for the whole church.

There were a few people quietly sitting or kneeling. On the left and right, halfway down the pews, he saw wooden booths with ornate, hefty, latticed doors and smaller latticed doors on each side. He thought, *Ah, the dreaded confessionals.* On the right side of the church, he saw a lady, wrinkled in clothes and skin, enter one of the booths. Others sat near the confessional, waiting; one older man was near the sanctuary at the front of the church, on his knees, gently rocking forward and back.

Only the confessional on the right side of the church was active, so he decided to investigate the unused one on the left, see if a few minutes alone in a priest's seat could help him feel more priestly for his role as Father Joseph. He stealthily entered the dark booth and closed the heavy door. He closed his eyes and tried to feel what a minister might feel.

Within a minute, someone entered the confessional and immediately began, "Bless me, Father, for I have sinned—"

"Wait a minute!" blurted Kurt.

The woman swiftly responded, "Father, I just got up the courage, I need to say this fast—God help me. I've been cheating on my husband."

Kurt was stunned. There he was, a nonpriest, a nonpracticing Catholic, a non-anything, acting like a priest, being confessed to. He felt trapped. In the silence, he heard the woman begin to cry. He girded himself and was compelled to speak, "Oh, dear, I can tell you are sorry. Is it over?"

"Yes, yes, Father. I was too guilty. It wasn't love. It wasn't what I thought. I couldn't keep lying and sneaking."

Kurt kept digging himself deeper because he couldn't seem to stop, but he seemed to be helping this poor woman dig out of her own pit. "It's obvious you are contrite. Uh, what should you do now?"

"I should go and sin no more," she replied.

"That's right," he said. "It was brave of you to come in, ah, um. God forgives you." Then he added, "Amen."

"That's it?" she asked.

"Yes, uh, that's it. Go. Be good."

The lady left slower than she had arrived, a little tentatively, but relieved of a heavy burden.

Kurt thought, *What just happened? That lady, surely, she is relieved. Free from her sin? I think so. But how could I?* Kurt felt elated. He felt a burning fever cover his body, and he seemed exhausted from this brief encounter. Was this a state of grace? He felt worried. He had just sort of forgiven her; had he given absolution? *I can't do that. But the woman. She thought she was, so was she? Was her confession valid? Did she confess but she wasn't forgiven?*

Before Kurt could resolve his inner dispute, another person entered the confessional.

"I'm closed," he said.

"Your closed? But this will only take a minute, Father."

Kurt quickly surmised that the old voice couldn't be much of a sinner, and it would only take a minute, so he took his second confession, "Okay, okay, make it quick."

The old person went through the rote beginning of her act of contrition then stated her sin, "Father, I'm beginning to lose faith that God exists."

"Cut," blurted the actor. "Whoa, dear, you said this would only take a minute. No, no. This confession is over. I want you to go to Mass, every day if you can, and pray for yourself. Fake it until you make it. Here you are at confession. Of course you believe. If you can't get to Mass, say a rosary. Then try confession again. Okay, dear, be on your way."

"Thank you, Father. I, I think you've saved me," she said, sobbing. "I love Our Lady of Victory. God bless you."

Kurt was again euphoric. He saved her. He gave her a penance. Again, his physical body was drained, exhausted. His head felt like it was on fire. At the risk of being visited again, he closed his eyes and tried to visualize a merciful God. The old acting method of visualizing, dreaming, letting your body and mind become the role seemed to take possession of him. As a confessor, he told a sinner to fake it until they make it. Acting. Role playing. Theatrics. His profession in film didn't seem to require much preparation. As an adventure action hero, he smiled or grimaced, said his rehearsed lines, and at a director's "Cut!" he had an opportunity for a redo if needed. A minister, on the other hand, had to perform more like a Broadway show, even a Broadway musical. They had to be ready and keep going no matter what, on the first take. This priestly stuff had no time for a redo. What a priest said in confession, or what his performance was on the altar, was raw acting, no director watching to cry out "Cut!"

This exhausted the Hollywood actor. He was in eternally deep water with no life preserver. What he said mattered. His improvisation as confessor zapped his strength. *How do priests do it? Are they really using supernatural assistance?* In the twenty minutes he spent sitting in the confessor's chair, he concluded his acting method wasn't good enough. He couldn't fake it, to be rescued by the director. There are no stunt doubles, no retakes in a confessional. This is the attitude he decided to take for his role as Father Joseph. He would take on a determined demeanor, fake the elation, fake the exhaustion, and endeavor to keep going, get everything right on the first take.

Kurt paused to forget acting and think about his father and God. He thought trying a little prayer for him wouldn't hurt. It wasn't that he hadn't believed in God; he simply led a life of dissipation. Live, let live, spend what he made, save for nothing, pause for nothing. He didn't take time to contemplate faith or what his father tried to teach him. In a world full of doubt, he bought into the idea of not considering any answers. The philosophy of seeing is believing was his easy way out. But now he found this ironic. As an actor he had used illusion and special effects to turn a world of make-believe into a world of suspended disbelief. It was how Stetson Stone had made his living time and time again. The church's smoke and scented incense used the same principle. It draws attention up, helps people believe, or suspends disbelief while working things out in hearts and minds. *Are the bells, the chants, the hymns attention-getters like a well-timed Broadway musical score? Are the robes of the priests and acolytes merely the costumes of an elaborate theater production?*

Now Kurt wondered why he was so adamantly resistant against his father. If the church was just smoke and mirrors, he ended up in a similarly illusionary profession. Maybe Kurt had been wrong. *How all-powerful is God? How can he be understood? Are angels real? Do supernatural persons really exist?* To put the world into an ordered place that humans could possibly understand required small minds to build props and costumes, songs, and cues.

Again, before Kurt could deeply figure out if he was praying or just trying to draw some logical conclusion, another person entered the confessional. Kurt thought, *Here we go again. I gotta get outta here.*

From the confessional, "Hello? Father?" The voice was male; someone sounding authoritative.

"Hello? May I help you?" Kurt replied.

"You keep making ladies cry. A couple of them are up at the Madonna statue sobbing and praying. Are you going to make me cry?"

"I certainly hope I won't make you cry. Confessions are over for today. You should come back tomorrow or another day. Someone, uh, qualified will be here."

"Father, what are you doing here? Will you take my confession or not?"

"I'm sorry," replied Kurt, "I won't. No more today. I have to leave. God bless you."

The man remained in the booth, in silence, and Kurt felt stuck, like he couldn't escape. Then the man began to quietly pray: "Oh, my Jesus, forgive us our sins. Save us from the fires of hell, lead all souls to heaven, especially those in most need of Your mercy."

Kurt replied, "What was that, sir? Can you repeat it?"

The man more firmly and loudly repeated it.

"That's me. I'm most in need of mercy," said Kurt.

"Yes, Father, I suppose so. Me too."

"No. No, please. Don't call me Father. I'm. I'm not a father."

"Hmm. That's what I suspected. I'm Father Raymond. You can call me Ray. Would you mind telling me what in God's green earth you are doing in my seat, making the church ladies cry?"

"Oh, god. I'm sorry. I. Well, I, I didn't mean to take any confessions but, but they just started blurting out, and I couldn't stop them, and I wanted to forgive them or for them to be forgiven, but I didn't have the power…"

"Okay, okay, sport. Slow down. Take a deep breath. Don't worry about the church ladies. They will recover from your scourging. With God all things are possible. Tell us about you."

Kurt inhaled deeply like catching his breath after sobbing. He explained how he got to where he was. Slowly, methodically, he explained more than how he took two confessions. Rather, he reached back to and before his acting career. He opened up in the security of the booth and the surprising calmness of Father Raymond to truly explain his nearly godless life. Father Raymond listened to one of the most thorough confessions he had received. Finally, when Kurt had purged himself of the burden of all his wrongs, Raymond told him he was absolved of all his sins.

"All my sins?"

"Yes, everything. Even stuff you don't remember. God forgives you thoroughly. Jesus died on the cross for this very moment. How does it feel to be in a state of grace?"

"I'm on fire. I'm burning up."

"Well, sport, you have come to the right place for that."

Kurt felt at home for the first time. He had much more to learn, but after a few years of discernment, and a few more in seminary, the great actor, the former Stetson Stone, performed his first Mass as Father Kurt at Our Lady of Victory Church.

About the Author

Timothy Jacques Maynard lives with his wife in Greene, Rhode Island. He is a native Rhode Islander, but he has travelled the world and lived in Ireland, Italy, Japan, and multiple states in America. He is a creative writer and prison chaplain but has been a naval officer, college professor, entrepreneur, college sailing coach, tour guide, and camp counselor. He holds a master of fine arts in creative writing from American College Dublin and also has a doctorate in educational leadership, a master of science in technology, and a master of arts in national security and strategic studies. He is a Knight of Malta. He has a charming wife and seven brothers and sisters as well as an extensive extended family.

www.ingramcontent.com/pod-product-compliance
Lightning Source LLC
LaVergne TN
LVHW040810131224
798956LV00012B/189

9798893151060